Journeys of The Dublin Trio

by

Dan McMeans

I want to dedicate this book to my wife for her years of devotion and love for me. Without her support and commitment as my best ally, this book would not be possible. She is both my best friend and a loving wife.

"Journeys of The Dublin Trio," by Dan McMeans ISBN 978-1-63868-219-6 (softcover).

Published 2025 by Virtualbookworm.com Publishing, P.O. Box 9949, College Station, TX 77842, US.

Contents

Introduction

Ryan Shamus is a former special operations Green Beret who served three tours of duty. He always had a strong faith in God and believed his discipline and focus came from his tours.

One day, he was walking down the path of Tookany Creek beside the creek and heard a slight whisper. "Look at me." At first, he wasn't sure where the voice was coming from, but he looked around his surroundings and he heard the voice again. "Look at me." He continued to look around, and then he realized the voice was coming from the setting sun in the west, and again he heard the voice. "Look at me."

And sure enough, the voice was coming from the sun as it was going down in the evening, and the sun was at a level of brightness that it did not hurt Ryan's eyes.

And the sun spoke to Ryan, and it said, "I am thy God, and I have chosen you to use your special set of skills to help people in all kinds of needs where they have lost hope. You will walk the plains just as your forefathers did to help bring hope where there is despair, as did Moses, Elijah, the Lord Jesus, and

Mother Teresa. You will work on donations, and I know that this life won't be financially rewarding, but your reward will be in my kingdom, which is the greatest treasure of all. You will go by the alias of the Dublin Trio, and the Trio in your name is to represent the Holy Trinity, which is the Father, the Son, and the Holy Ghost. Carry on, and I love you."

Ryan stood there quivering because he had just realized that the almighty God had just spoken to him as the sun went down behind the mountain in the park. Ryan was still standing, quivering and wiping tears from his face. As God talked to him, he felt great love and warmth from the sun, touching him with grace. With his hands shaking, he gathered himself, knowing what he had to do because he was a man of God, and a lot of work had to be done for him to glorify God.

Ryan Shamus set up his webpage, got a fax machine and business cards, and made himself available to people with various needs.

Uprising at Lawndale Elementary School

This is the story of many students who actually existed in Lawndale Elementary School. They traveled through grades one through six together and were close friends.

There were about ten students in sixth grade at Lawndale Elementary School who thought it would be cool to spend the night in the school, so they devised a plan for each of them to tell their parents that all of them would be spending the night at each other's house to make sure they had an alibi for the night. The ten students in question hid in the closet room at the back of one of the classes as the staff left the school for the day.

So the students had the school to themselves for the night. They pooled their money from allowances together and ordered a couple of pizzas, which was the typical thing twelve-year-olds do when they got together. As the night went on, they played the games Life and Monopoly, and the playful but harmless game Spin the Bottle.

They decided to tell ghost stories as the night fell. Chills, thrills, and laughs followed as the stories went into the night, until a sudden shift in temperature occurred, and then the students noticed the hair on their forearms started to rise, to their alarm.

One of the girls remembered from a movie she watched that when evil is present, the hair will rise on your forearms, and a temperature shift to a cooler climate could also happen. These twelve-year-olds knew something about togetherness, because they had all been together since first grade.

One of the boys stood up and said, "We've been together for a long time, and we can't panic now. There must be a reason why this is happening to us. Let's put our thoughts together and try to unravel what's happening."

The students knew they were up against evil, but for what purpose? So they thought maybe there were answers in the past, buried in the school's history.

The honor roll of former teachers in the main hallway went back to 1914, from when the school was constructed, so the students thought that was a good place to start. Every picture had to be examined, and every possible detail of the ten pictures on the wall had to be looked at and exhausted.

Hence, as the students went down the aisle, separating their responsibilities by dividing into two teams of five, they scrutinized each picture. One of the teams found a peculiar photo of a woman teacher in front of a fireplace with a vase behind her on the mantle. As the students examined the language on the vase, they noticed it was a language they had never seen before.

The students wanted an image of this language. They knew the teachers used a Polaroid camera occasionally to take a picture of the student of the month. Hence, they went to the teacher's closet, found the Polaroid camera, brought it back to the teacher from 1914, and took a picture of her with her vase of this mysterious language. They took the picture to the school's computer and tried to look up the language.

After exhausting many past languages, the students came across writings that were very similar to the writings on the vase. That language was called "Abyssal" texts, and to the students' shock, the origins of these writings came from evil.

One of the girls expressed her thoughts above the surprised chatter. "Everybody stay calm. Let's connect the pieces and see what it all means."

The students googled the teacher's name and learned that she was married to an iron maker from that time. Unbeknownst to the students, the teacher had her husband hand-make an artifact to the specifications and guidance from generations of passed-down evil wisdom. This artifact was specifically created for the future to bring in a significant abundant evil energy based on the design along with the spectrum and elements that would coalesce at a future date. And this future date happened to be the same as the Lawndale students staying overnight.

What the students didn't realize was that Satan sent a demon to the school to help harness the ultimate evil power of this artifact, and that was what they were experiencing. Realizing that this was getting a little beyond them, and thinking they could use some help, they went to the school computer, found someone in the area who had expertise, and sent an urgent message to the Dublin Trio to please come to their aid and help them with this situation.

About an hour later, the Dublin Trio arrived at Lawndale Elementary School to the delight of the Lawndale students, and they let him in and gave him an update on all that was going on with them. The students at the school had a library in which they did homework. So they went to the library with the information they had at hand and started to look into the ancient writing of "Abyssal" to see if they could find any clues.

Then, the Dublin Trio and the students turned their attention to the picture again to see if they could get any more clues from it. They started to analyze everything in the picture, making sure no small detail was left behind. One of the boys noticed the bracelet looked like a blue sapphire stone.

Still, if they looked closely at three separate areas of the bracelet containing small black gems with the numbers nine, nine, nine, it all seemed decorative when you looked at the bracelet as a whole, but there it was in three different spots. What could this mean? Was it a clue? The students and the Trio wondered.

Because this was a numerical equation, and the students and the Dublin trio knew by then the teacher and her origins of evil, the next question was what did these numbers have to do with evil. Hence, the Dublin

Trio and the students went to the school computer and did some searching, and this was what they found.

In number theory, an evil number is a non-negative integer whose evil number is the number of ones in its binary representation. "Evil" is also used to describe certain mathematical constants, such as the Ramanujan theory, a mathematician of his time. He noticed that evil constants in math were the sum of the digits 666.

One of the students brought to their attention that 999 could be 666 upside-down, which could be a clue. That was an incredible revelation. They all thought, let's go deeper into the school computer, find out if her original desk was still in the school, and examine it.

Sure enough, her desk was still there, and the Lawndale students and the Dublin Trio went to further their investigation. They arrived in her original classroom, but as they started to examine the desk, they noticed a temperature shift in the room, as the hairs on their forearms and necks rose.

The Dublin Trio said, "Do not be afraid, but I think someone is here with us." He went into the middle of the classroom and boldly said, "We are not afraid of your evil tactics to try to stop us, for we embody the glory of God and his sovereignty against evil."

Then the demon, with the guidance of Satan, picked up chalk and wrote on the chalkboard, "Then you will die."

The Dublin Trio, in defiance, went back up to the chalkboard, erased the demon's message, and wrote,

"We will feel no evil for though art with me. I trust in the Lord, for there is our anchor and our faith, which will always be our guidance for our salvation."

They turned their attention to continue examining the desk and found a secret chamber with a three-digit code. They entered the code 666, and the chamber opened. They found a metallic statue of a man with arms stretched above his head, holding the Earth upside-down. The man had a peculiar necklace on him, and they Googled its shape and look. It was the Devil's Eye Necklace.

They knew this statue had significance to the whole situation and had to be destroyed, so they concluded the statue must be put into the school's coal furnace, where metal could be melted, and that was what they did.

The Dublin Trio and the students took the statue down to the cellar. While heading down, the demon tried to scare them by rattling things around the stairs as they walked. Still, they finally arrived, turned on the furnace, and the Dublin Trio said a prayer.

"From the point of light within the Mind of God, let light stream forth into the minds of men. Let light descend on earth. From the point of love within the heart of God, let love stream into the hearts of every person, every being. Let love descend on earth. May Jesus, the world teacher, return to earth. From the center where the will of God is known, let purpose guide the will of every person, every being, the purpose that the Holy Masters know and serve. Let goodwill and the will to do good descend on earth. From the center, which we call the human race, let the plan of love and light work outward. And may it seal the door where evil dwells."

Then, the Trio tossed the evil statue into the furnace, and the ten students and the Trio started to plan a trap for the demon. As they presented different ideas to each other, one female student said, "Why can't we use the Star of Bethlehem? It's the brightest star in the sky."

"True," said the Dublin Trio. "We can lure the demon out into the courtyard and pray to Jesus to empower the Star of Bethlehem to come to our aid."

So, the students and the Dublin Trio went about the plan of taunting the demon in the main hallway by grabbing the evil teacher's picture, putting it on the floor and stomping on it, and bellowing to the demon to see if he would show up. And sure enough, he did. They knew they demon had arrived by the familiar characteristics of how the room changed in temperature and the hair rose on their forearms and necks.

They knew if they started to run, the demon would follow, so they ran down the corridor, out the doors of Lawndale Elementary School, into the courtyard, and looked into the sky at the brilliant Star of Bethlehem. The students and the Trio prayed, led by one of the students, who was an altar boy.

"Lord, you are our refuge and our fortress. Please bless the Star of Bethlehem to come to our aid and protect us from the evil forces that try to undermine your faith. Amen."

Suddenly, as they looked at the Star of Bethlehem in the sky, it was activated with swirling energy. Then, like a lightning bolt, came a stream of energy from the star onto the courtyard as if it was pursuing the demon. As it caught up to the demon, they saw the stream of energy illuminate the creature. It was not a pretty sight to see. The demon struggled and tried to escape, and then he finally vaporized into thin air, and the stream of energy from the Star of Bethlehem returned to its glory.

Then the Dublin Trio knelt, and the ten students and the Trio embraced for a group hug. The Dublin Trio said maybe it was fate that the collection of their friendship decided to spend the night at the school, because God works his mysteries in wonderous ways.

The Lost City of Gold

The Dublin Trio received a fax request to help an independent excavation company because planes with sonar had detected a deep cavern in the hills of Colombia, where they thought the El Dorado, the lost city of gold, existed.

El Dorado is considered a mystical city of gold in South America, inspired by the Muisca tribe, who were indigenous to that area. The theory is that gold was very prevalent in that area, and the Muisca, which existed over two thousand years ago, was proud to have abundant gold. However, when Spanish conquistadors heard these tales, they pursued this place of plentiful gold and precious stones, and they began a conquest to invade and take the gold for themselves, as legend tells the story.

So the Dublin Trio gathered his things and took the next plane to meet with the independent excavation company that hired him to find this cavern. The Dublin Trio touched down in South America, where the only way to get to the hills of Guinea in Colombia, where the Andes Mountains are located, was to go through thick brush as you climbed a mountain to arrive where the Muisca tribe resided.

As the Dublin Trio was moving through the thick brush, chopping with his machete to create a path before him, he suddenly came across a clearing with a small hut and a woman sitting outside of it on a log. The Dublin Trio was mystified by the woman and the hut in the middle of the brush.

The woman motioned to the Dublin Trio. She said, "Do not be frightened by my surroundings. I am a traveler on this planet searching for the answers to our existence as we go through the trials and errors of our evolution. I am known in this area as a tree interpreter and psychic, and I have learned to communicate with all the trees that inhabit this area. I can pick up their vibes to guide me. Please come closer. I'm hopeful you will join me for tea."

The Dublin Trio, who always wanted to engage and learn from people in his travels, agreed to join this woman for a cup of tea. They discussed her gifts as she went on. "Trees can communicate with each other through an underground network, sharing resources and sending signals, and they can also send airborne chemicals. They have a low vibrational consciousness that is different from ours. I have learned to interpret their vibes, but I'm also a psychic."

The tree interpreter woman did a Tarot reading on the Dublin Trio, and while reading the cards, the Tower card came up. The psychic woman was concerned for the Dublin Trio because the Tower represents danger, crisis, sudden change, and destruction. The psychic expressed her deep concern, and the Dublin Trio took it wisely and thanked her for the tea before he proceeded on his quest to the Guinea hills of Colombia to find the lost city of gold, El Dorado.

The Dublin Trio continued up the incline through heavy brush with his machete until he came to a clearing he thought was a good spot to pitch his tent for the night. Since he was a former Green Beret, he had survivalist skills. Once the tent was up, he decided to build a cozy fire for himself. Then, he started to think about life and what the woman said – that we are all travelers on this planet, pursuing the same thing.

There were many theories as to why humans were asked to do time on Earth before returning to the afterlife. The Dublin Trio contemplated what the tree psychic said. He believed that possibly we were all here on Earth to go through trials and sacrifices, and to use reflection to understand that we're always looking for opportunities to evolve as humans and become better people as we go through life. Hopefully, by the time we reached the end of our lives, we have confronted our shortcomings and became a better person, and go back to our maker with more wholeness.

The next morning, the Dublin Trio gathered his things and continued his journey. As he was going through the brush, the dense foliage of the Guinea hills closed in around him. Sunlight flickered through the leaves, casting dappled shadows on the forest floor. He maneuvered cautiously, the scent of damp earth mingling with the faint sweetness of wildflowers.

Suddenly, a rustle echoed from the underbrush. The ground shifted beneath him. Before he could react, a massive anaconda lunged, its coils wrapping tightly around his right leg.

"Get off me, you beast!" He grunted, struggling against the serpent's grip. The snake tightened, its scales warm and slick against his skin. He planted his feet, channeling every ounce of strength. "Not today!" he shouted, twisting his body. With a fierce yank, he freed his leg, twisting to face the creature. The anaconda lunged again, jaws wide, but he sidestepped.

"Come on then!" He lunged forward, his blade slicing through the air. The snake hissed, a sound like wind through dry leaves. In a final, desperate move, he grabbed the snake's jaw, forcing it open. With one swift motion, he drove the knife deep. The anaconda thrashed, then fell still. Breathing heavily, he wiped sweat from his brow.

The Dublin Trio thought back to what the tree interpreter woman said about danger in his surroundings in his future, and he was sure it must have been this snake that appeared out of nowhere.

He reached the peak of the Guinea hills, where he met the owner of the independent excavation company. They discussed the Dublin Trio's mission and where the sonar planes picked up the hidden cavern. The Dublin Trio looked at the situation, the logistics, and what was schematically involved. He got his gear together to harness and rappel down into the cavern, a two-hundred-foot descent that only a highly experienced rappeler could accomplish.

The Dublin Trio reached the end of his descent, and to his surprise, there was a pile of gold bricks at the end. While he was looking over the bricks, within them was a leather pouch containing a written note from the Muisca tribe. He secured the leather pouch with his possessions and ascended back up the independent excavation company to let them know that he'd found gold.

Once at the top, the Dublin Trio and the owner of the excavation company brought in an interpreter who was in the area to transcribe the note. It said, "We are the Muisca Tribe. We love our community, and we would like you to respect our hard work and how we went about harvesting this gold. We understood the value of gold, and we respected it. We want whoever discovers this gold to respect it as well, because we know in our communities how something of such purity as gold can be misused if it is not respected."

The Dublin Trio and the independent excavator were moved by a message from two thousand years ago, left by a very knowledgeable and wise tribe. With wealth comes responsibility, and this was what the Muisca Tribe was trying to teach us.

The Passageway

A young couple bought a beautiful old house that was about two hundred years old in Montgomery County, Pennsylvania. Soon after they moved in, they were assessing the furniture in their master bedroom and wanted to move one of the bureaus. So they collectively attempted to push it aside because it was significantly heavy.

After they moved the bureau, they noticed a five-foot door that was right behind it. So they jointly opened the door and entered the walkable passageway beyond. They were astonished that this secret passageway was in their home, so they continued until it came to an end and looked around. They saw a trap door, so they opened it, and they both had to crawl through the passable crawl space beyond. They were wondering where it was leading to when they came to another trap door that led into a room.

So, they pivoted into the room. This was perplexing to them. The room had only a wooden table and a chair, with a chandelier above the table that looked like the original one that came with the house. The husband thought to himself, there must be some clue in this room to help understand what's going on.

They thought the legs of the table might be hollow, and the husband was willing to untangle any possible hints. He started to unscrew each leg and investigate the hollow parts, and to his surprise, he found a note inside one. "I am the original nanny of this house. This was my special room where I sought refuge for all the worshipers of Christ. I was anointed the role of nanny to protect this house when the Prince of Darkness built it."

They were both horrified by this, as it was very unsettling news about the origins of the home. Nevertheless, the husband wanted to address every area of the room. He started to look at everything, including the chandelier. He estimated the chandelier's mounting plate was about eighteen inches in diameter, which he thought was large. In comparison, the standard mounting plate would be six to twelve inches.

He took his Swiss army knife, unscrewed the plate, looked at the ceiling, and found another note. The note read, "I am the original gardener of this house, and I observed a lot of evil doings. I tried my best to help the families that lived here, and here's my warning that the original nanny the house came with was evil. I don't know where she came from, but she was evil. I also feel the grandfather clock's chimes are harmful to people, but I can't prove it."

The couple returned to the master bedroom with all this information. They were astonished at what was revealed, and now they were going to put together a master plan on how to get beyond this because they didn't want to move out of the house. They wanted to resolve the situation.

The husband went to the library and researched the house, trying to dig up as much information as he could on its history. The house was two hundred years old and must have had some history relating to it.

The husband started looking at landmasses of polarity and duality. He realized the house was built based on the mathematical and geological axes where evil centralized. It was built on top of the evil energy vortex, which was possibly why the place was haunted. As he looked through the house's history, he saw there had been five unexplained deaths in the house.

So, the husband went home and discussed the situation with his wife, and they both considered things as if they felt this was their home. They felt strongly about the principle of "Home is where the heart is," and they agreed it would be their cornerstone of addressing this issue. Because at the center of it all was the foundation of love, they felt it was their destiny to face this challenge together. But they agreed to bring in someone to advise them.

The Dublin Trio was at his home, and he noticed on his web page that a young couple had contacted him, wanting him to come out to Montgomery County to help them investigate a possible haunted house with unexplained deaths throughout its two-hundred-year history. He contacted the young couple and made arrangements to drive out to see them.

As the Dublin Trio entered the driveway of the young couple's home, he noticed two gargoyles flanking the entrance of the driveway as he pulled up to the front of the house. He entered the house, met the young couple, sat down to listen to them, and tried to assess the situation. He heard the husband describe the nature of both notes left in the secret room.

Hence, the Dublin Trio got up to thoroughly examine the grandfather clock. He looked way back in the corner, where there was a small box. The box contained a finger cut off from the top knuckle up to the fingernail. The Trio returned to his chair to look at the finger, gather his thoughts, and determine his next course of action.

Maybe there was another clue in the cabinet of the grandfather clock. The Trio reexamined the space, and attached to the top of the cabinetry, he found another note. It read, "I am the gardener, and I got into an altercation with the nanny because I knew she was up to no good. In my battle with her, I cut off her finger, which is in this grandfather clock."

Realizing the impact of the note, he walked back to his chair to sit down to analyze the situation. He opened up the box to look at the finger and had an idea to see if there was any history relating to the fingerprint. He got the fingerprint tested, and when the results came in, they revealed the nanny was raised in a nearby orphanage.

So, the Dublin Trio was off to dig up some information from the orphanage, and the husband asked if he could tag along as his is a nurse practitioner in genetics. The Trio was more than willing to have him come along. They arrived at the orphanage and told the secretary their issue, but the secretary was resistant to reveal any confidential information.

The Trio revealed his credentials as a former Green Beret, trying to convey the urgency of the situation, and the secretary then gave the nanny's mother's name. Through more research, the husband and the Trio found she was buried at Oakmont Cemetery, located in nearby Bucks County. Oakmont is an, old abandoned cemetery.

The Trio and the husband went there, found the coffin, and opened the casket, which revealed a woman still in her day dress, but she had hairy arms and hair on her face. It was a very perplexing, confusing moment for the Trio and the husband. Suddenly, they realized they were surrounded by many crows looking at them and knew they had to hurry. The husband said, "Wait! Let me take a DNA sample, and we'll get it examined."

Consequently, the husband and the Trio arrived at the husband's DNA facility and prepared the DNA for testing. They received the results, but it was too complex for the husband to understand. So, they sent the results to a forensic DNA analyst. It came back with a molecule breakdown of the nanny's mother's DNA, which was werewolf in nature. It had a unique set of genes in place for the production of specific proteins responsible for tissue changes, muscle mass, and potential bone structure modifications, which allowed it shapeshifting ability.

This DNA threw them for a loop. Werewolves were not human, and they were created from evil. The nanny was raised for a mission of evil.

The Dublin Trio focused on the five unexplained deaths in the house during the last two hundred years. He started to think about what the gardener said about the chimes polluting the good people in the house, and the Trio investigated what hours of the day were associated with evil. He discovered that 2:00 A.M. was called the devil's hour, and consequently, the grandfather clock chimed on that hour more than any other.

And the Dublin Trio was convinced these chimes had rhythmically evil sounds that corrupted the minds of people who had lived here, causing them to do harmful things to other people. He knew what he needed to do. He went to the trunk of his car, removed an axe, and returned to the house to face the grandfather clock. He had to chop up the clock so it would never harm anyone again.

As he approached the grandfather clock, Satan was watching from afar and didn't want the grandfather clock destroyed, so he sped up the big hand on the clock until it hit 2:00 in the morning when the evil chimes were at their peak, trying to corrupt the mind of the Dublin Trio. But the Dublin Trio's mind was disciplined from his years as a Green Beret, and he was able to withstand the rhythmic, corruptive evil sounds of the chimes.

He composed himself to continue the march forward, and then raised his axe and took a mighty swing at the grandfather clock, hacking a gaping hole in its side. And then, the Trio saw one luminous figure after another float out of the grandfather clock, like mists in human form. Could these be the souls of those who died unexplained deaths, like the Dublin Trio thought? As the luminous figures walked past the Trio, they turned and looked back to thank him for releasing their souls. And the Dublin Trio continued to chop up the grandfather clock to ensure it would never be used again for evil purposes.

This story began because the young couple believed the home is where the heart is. The cornerstone of that message is love, which can propel you to amazing things when you consider that love is the foundation of all building blocks for humanity's purpose.

The Mirror's Gate

There was a very clairvoyant boy, fine-tuned with the finer senses of his being, and wise beyond his years. This boy was misunderstood as he grew up in Stanleywood, Pennsylvania, in a tree-lined neighborhood in the northern corridor. Nearby, there were regional locomotive tracks. One day, he got into an argument with his mother. He stormed out of the house, went down to the tracks, and started walking on them.

Because he was not paying attention, the townsfolk got worried along with his mom as they watched from a distance. A passenger train was heading right for him as he walked toward it. It was alarming how close he was getting to the passenger train, and the townsfolk and his mom were too far away to help him.

Suddenly, to everybody's surprise, a gust of wind came through the fields and over the embankment, picked up this little boy by the armpits, and moved him off the train tracks right before the train was going to hit him. The townsfolk and the mom were astonished because it looked like an intervention, and news spread among the neighborhood that maybe the gift came from above, which caused much whispering.

Now, the boy was twelve years old, and he had continued down the path of enlightenment. His mom was going about her business around the house, cleaning, and she heard her son playing the piano in the living room. The little boy's name was Luke. Unbeknownst to him, the mirror above the piano had a sinister dimension that had been dormant for all these years. It came alive and suddenly captured Luke while playing the piano, drawing him into the mirror.

In the meantime, his mom, who had been cleaning the upstairs, suddenly realized that Luke had stopped playing the piano. She thought it was mysterious that he was right in the middle of a beautiful song and just stopped. She decided to investigate and went down to where the piano was. To her surprise, Luke wasn't around. She looked all over the place and couldn't find him. She searched outside the house, then went back in, calling Luke's name, and then returned to the piano. On top of the piano, she found Luke's toy pistol, which he wore around his waist.

She found this very perplexing. So, when her husband came home that night, they put their heads together to create the best comprehensive plan to find their son. They called the local authorities, the police, to let them know that their son was missing, but they also went online to hire an independent person with expertise, and that was the Dublin Trio.

The Dublin Trio received an urgent message from Luke's mom, saying Luke was missing. He contacted Luke's parents and arranged to meet them in a couple of days to investigate this situation in Stanleywood, Pennsylvania, which was past Bradford.

The Dublin Trio arrived at the house, met the parents, and started investigating the situation. There wasn't much information except a toy pistol, which had been on Luke's hip, left on top of the piano. The police thoroughly searched the house and couldn't find anything. The Dublin Trio went to work, painstakingly looking at every angle and every detail, narrowing their focus on the mirror because the toy pistol was on top of the piano.

It looked like a natural trajectory, but as bizarre as it may have seemed, the Trio wanted to exhaust every scenario. He observed the large, old mirror above the piano, taking in every detail from all angles. To his surprise, he found an engraving on the side of the mirror that said Count Victor Kingsley.

The Dublin Trio approached the mom about the engraving, and the mom wasn't aware of it, but knew of the family's ancestral name and said she only knew the tall tales relating to his name. She still had his family journal, which she never opened up.

What she knew of him was that he was the count to a king who was deeply into mysticism. This king took a strange twist by looking at the darker side, as he was more intrigued by the dark forces. He commissioned Count Victor Kingsley to look into that. Then, the count came to worship and respect the values of the dark side.

The mom entered the attic, found Count Victor's journal, and brought it down so the Dublin Trio could to see if he could find any clues. The Dublin Trio looked through the journal. To his astonishment, he found information about this family's mirror from five hundred years ago. Count Victor Kingsley discussed in his journal how he used the dark forces of black magic to curse the mirror to create a sinister dimension beyond the glass.

With this in hand, the Dublin Trio walked to the mirror in the living room and thought if there was evil dark energy in there, and he believed Luke was somehow captured and drawn into this mirror, it was his job to get him out. The Dublin Trio knew something about evil energy. He was firm in his faith.

He positioned himself in front of the mirror and insulted and disrespected the forces of evil inside for thinking they were superior to men. Suddenly, the Dublin Trio saw a subtle variance of energy change on the mirror glass, suggesting a welcoming gesture to test his faith. He walked up, took the ashtray off the piano top, and threw it into the mirror. It disappeared as if the dimension beyond the mirror had swallowed up the ashtray.

The Dublin Trio was convinced the boy was in some sinister mirror dimension, and he decided to go in after him.

In the meantime, Luke knew he was in an ominous, sinister world but soon found a lot of toys suited for a boy his age. "Do you like the toys I provided for you?" a voice that came out of thin air asked.

"Who are you?"

"I am the giver of power, born from greed."

"Isn't greed not good for you?"

"Some of the most powerful men on Earth are born from greed."

"But God describes greed as selfish ambition."

"God is delusional about many things. I can help you understand a bigger, better picture.

"You think God's power is delusional? Only the Anti-Christ would feel like that."

"Who are you to question me? I promise you, you will see the powers of my darkness."

Luke then ran down the path because he realized that he'd just had dialogue with the Prince of Darkness. He did what any little boy would do, which was to seek and find. He came to a cliff's edge, where he could do some soul-searching on what to do next.

Then, as if out of the sky, a luminous particle-energy resonation appeared before him with wings that looked like an angel, and it spoke to him. "I am the archangel Michael, and I'm here to help you. I would like you to climb down about twenty-five feet, and you will see a cavern on the side of this cliff where you can seek safety and protection from the environment. When you reach the cavern, I would like you to look for an old wooden chest and open it. You will find an old gold crucifix necklace that was once worn by King Arthur, who loved God very much. I'm going to bless this crucifix, which will help protect you against the powers of darkness."

Luke climbed down the mountain and did what the angel instructed him to do. He found the cavern and wooden chest, opened the chest, and saw a beautiful old gold crucifix necklace worn by King Arthur, who presided over the Knights of the Round Table.

With the necklace came a note that read, "I am King Arthur, and this crucifix necklace is essential to me. I've worn it as a symbol to demonstrate of my love for my God but to also demonstrate with that love comes courage and bravery, which embodies the discipline that comes when you believe in your faith and your convictions. For what is a man without his principles? A man gets his principles from his faith, and this is what propels him forward in life. That's why I want to share this necklace with whomever finds it, in the hope they carry on the destiny and fortitude of what my faith meant to me."

After Luke read this note, he then saw a mystical, glowing energy essence descend. It appeared to bless the crucifix, which Archangel Michael said he would do. The boy picked up the crucifix necklace and wore it proudly around his neck.

Luke stayed in the cavern for several days with his crucifix for safety. While he was resting, a voice again spoke to him out of thin air. It said, "Do you think that crucifix is going to protect you against me?"

Realizing who it was, Luke stood and said, "I am proud of my heritage of courageous people who went before me in the name of their faith, and I'm not going to let them down." He then climbed down the rest of the cliff to the bottom and took off down the path, where he came across a pet cemetery. It looked like the same cemetery his beloved childhood dog was buried in. Luke could not believe his eyes, but he proceeded to look for his beloved childhood dog's gravestone.

He found it and started to pay respects to the dog he loved so much, and then he heard mocking laughing from thin air. Luke, who was wise beyond his years for a twelve-year-old boy, knew then the dark forces had fooled him and that this pet cemetery was an illusion. Just as he thought that, he witnessed six menacing figures that looked like Doberman pinschers growing from a distance, and it scared him.

He decided to run down the path, but the Dobermans pursued him until he was trapped by the cliff. He didn't have enough time to climb back up before the dogs attacked him. He braced himself for the worst. Then, suddenly, six large bucks with huge antlers jumped in front of Luke to fend off the dogs. The Dobermans knew they were no match for the bucks and their antlers with the heads set in a fighting position, antlers ready for battle. It was too much, and the dogs withdrew.

In the meantime, the Dublin Trio had been walking around in this evil dimension, calling out Luke's name. He found footprints that led to the top of the cliff and assumed Luke went down there. He rappelled down the cliff, continuing to call Luke's name until Luke heard him.

Luke came running after the bucks saved him with their antlers to see this heroic-looking man. The Dublin Trio embraced him and explained to Luke that he was hired to bring him back. The Dublin Trio returned him to where he had first arrived from the mirror's gate. Once there, he looked around, investigated his surroundings, and looked for a way to get back to Luke's house. He came upon a bush and saw something odd worth investigating. Sure enough, it was the way back to Luke's house. The Dublin Trio and Luke passed through the portal and ended up back in the living room at Luke's home, safe and sound.

Luke's mother thanked the Dublin Trio for saving her son. Naturally, the Dublin Trio was humbled by her compliment because he was doing his job. He knelt to talk to Luke because he knew the boy had a gift from above. He told Luke, "You're going to be tested in many ways as you grow older. As you continue your studies in the wisdom of your spirituality, remember always to pray, because that will be your guide and connection to the pathway of your greatest potential."

The Russian Insurrection

Ryan Shamus was a former Green Beret in the special forces unit who now went by his alias, the Dublin Trio. With his unique skills, he helped people who had lost hope. The Trio in his name represented the Father, the Son, and the Holy Ghost.

The Dublin Trio was in North Carolina, vacationing. He was in a bait shop and overheard several guys talking at the other end of the counter. They were talking about something very alarming, which was forty Russian soldiers going through infantry drills up in the hills of North Carolina.

Being a former Green Beret, the Dublin Trio approached the two men and inquired about the situation. The men confirmed they saw about 40 Russian soldiers doing infantry drills, and the Trio wanted to see it for himself. He asked the guys for a geographical location.

The next morning, the Dublin Trio got up early and went to that location. He couldn't believe his eyes when he saw the Russian soldiers there. Something had to be done about this. *Under no circumstances can we allow this,* he said to himself. He called his old commander, who was retired, and told him the news, and the commander was alarmed as well. He promised the Trio that he would look into it.

The commander investigated the situation and contacted the commander of the Russian Infantry Squad. They met, and the meeting was cordial. The commander of the Russian team told the former U.S. commander that they were here legally on a temporary resident visa. The U.S. commander happened to have his own infantry militia and entered into a friendly wager between his group and the Russian commander's group for war games.

"The wager that I would like to propose is if that if my territorial army defeats your infantry in a friendly game, with a former U.S. diplomat being an impartial judge, your infantry will have to leave our country peacefully. If we lose, my organized militia members will clean and polish your soldiers' boots with spit and shine."

The commander of the Russian infantry group thought about it and revealed to the U.S. commander that he would accept the terms of the agreement. He said, "I look forward to your militia reserve cleaning and polishing my soldiers' boots," and the U.S. commander leaned forward and said, "We'll see!"

Both sides agreed that the games would be governed by the principles of war and the law of armed conflict, also known as the law of war. These principles ensure that war games are conducted ethically and within the bounds of international law. They would be judged by a former diplomat from the U.S. embassy, who had pledged to be impartial under international law. Let the games begin.

The sun hung low in the North Carolina sky, casting long shadows over the rolling hills. The air buzzed with anticipation, a mix of the scent of pine and the faint whir of helicopters in the distance. On one side stood the U.S. militia members, clad in camo and bravado, their squinting eyes scanning the horizon. Opposite them, the Russian soldiers, equally determined, adjusted their gear, their accents thick and their expressions steely.

"Gentlemen," the U.S. commander began, his voice steady. "Today's game is simple. We conquer that hill." He pointed to the ridge that loomed in the distance, bathed in the orange glow of sunset. "And the stakes are high."

"High enough for vodka?" a Russian soldier quipped, his laughter rolling like thunder through the tense air.

"Enough for a one-way ticket home if you lose," the commander shot back, his voice low but firm. The challenge hung between them, heavy and electric.

The Russian commander stepped forward, arms crossed. "If we lose, we'll leave. But should you fall, your men will polish our boots until the sun rises." His smile was sharp, a wolf baring its teeth.

"Deal," the U.S. commander replied, a grin on his face. The militia members hooted and hollered, their excitement palpable.

As the two sides moved into position, the hills erupted into a cacophony of shouts, commands, and the soft thud of boots against the earth. The U.S. militia advanced, weaving through trees and underbrush, their movements synchronized like a well-oiled machine.

"Go, go! Push forward!" a militia member barked, adrenaline surging through his veins. The sound of branches snapping underfoot echoed in the otherwise still air. "C'mon, boys! Let's show them how it's done!" another shouted, laughter bubbling amidst the tension.

Further up the hill, a Russian soldier aimed, his breath steady. "They think they can take us so easily. We'll show them." He pressed the trigger, the shot ringing out swift and sharp.

"Incoming!" a militia member yelled, ducking just in time. The sound of the bullet whizzed past, a reminder of the stakes at play.

The game escalated, a dance of strategy and stealth. The U.S. militia crested a ridge, their eyes lighting up as they spotted the Russian flag fluttering atop a nearby peak. "Charge!" their commander shouted, a rallying cry that pierced through the chaos.

"Not so fast!" a Russian soldier yelled, scrambling to defend their position. The clash intensified, shouts blending with the rustle of leaves and the thud of bodies against the earth. An explosion rocked the ground, sending dirt and debris flying.

"Get down!" someone yelled, laughter mingling with the thrill of battle. Finally, after what felt like an eternity of skirmishing, the U.S. militia surged forward, taking the hill with a triumphant roar. "Victory!" they howled, their voices echoing through the forest.

The Russian soldiers, though defeated, maintained their composure, shoulders squared. "We'll be back," one called out, a hint of respect in his tone despite the loss.

The U.S. commander met his gaze with a smirk on his lips. "Next time, try not to bring a knife to a gunfight." The stakes had been settled as the sun dipped below the horizon, but the promise of future encounters lingered like smoke in the air.

The Dublin Trio spent the night at the U.S. commander's militia members' base and rose the next morning with the militia. They raised the American flag, and at morning taps, the Dublin Trio saluted the flag for what it stood for and all the sacrifices that took place for our liberties. A new day had dawned in pursuit of a more perfect union.

The Lost Civilization of Atlantis

The Dublin Trio went to the library for some good reading material. He found a book that looked like it hadn't been read in a while, so he blew the dust off the front of the book and skimmed the contents, realizing these were true stories of pirates of the past. He came across one story that he thought was intriguing, called, "The Sixth Sense of the Captain's Cat."

The Dublin Trio went on to read the story of Captain Calico Jack, a pirate who discovered one of the remnants of the lost civilization of Atlantis in 1600. He found a cave near the Strait of Gibraltar with a lab that was untouched for thousands of years. The civilization of Atlantis was known to be very advanced for their time. Captain Calico Jack found many quartz crystals, and there were instructions left behind on how to handle the crystals because they could augment power.

The note, which was by the antennas, said, "We are the people of Atlantis. We are leaving behind our discoveries and learnings of quartz crystals. We are hopeful that it helps to move mankind forward in its quest to understand our connection to nature better."

Captain Calico Jack laughed at this notion but was fascinated with the power of the quartz crystals. He had his men gather them and take them to his ship. He followed the instructions, and his crew figured out how to use the crystals to augment power to their turbine, which increased propulsion.

Captain Calico Jack was responsible for four ships, marauders of the high seas. They used the quartz crystals to their advantage for theft and thievery, but something very unusual was happening. The captain's cat had an unusual awareness about her, almost as if she had a sixth sense, as she witnessed and saw all the unforgivable things the captain, her owner, advocated. The captain and his four ships had this advanced propulsion, which gave them a substantial competitive advantage, and when they boarded the other vessels, they vandalized them and stole their belongings. This was the pirate way of life.

The captain's cat, whose name was Musket, was very aware and knew the difference between right and wrong. Then, one day, Captain Calico and his four ships came face to face with the British Navy, which also had four ships, and all the ships were equipped with cannons. The British Navy opened fire first, sending its cannon balls billowing and blistering onto Captain Calico's vessels. Just when the captain was going to give the command to return fire, Musket, who was aware of all the marauding and thievery, wanted to disrupt the process. So, she jumped out of the captain's arms and onto the tables with all the navigation maps.

This angered the captain, but Musket kept jumping around, table to table, hoping to delay the order to respond. Finally, the captain captured Musket and lifted his hand to strike her for punishment. Suddenly, his sailors came rushing into his cabin telling him of a thirty-foot ethereal and transparent goddess-like woman emerging from the ocean.

And she said, "I am Yemaya, the Ocean Goddess. Do not strike that cat! We have observed pirates long enough to know that you are an unjust culture, and you need to change your ways. We would like you to use your love of the high seas as a force of nature in seeing things in a different light, knowing that all positive things come from nature, as a future mystic once foretold. Change how you look at things, and what you look at will change. I leave you with peace. Captain Calico, Musket is a very special cat, and she is aware beyond her senses. She helped you in many ways today."

The Dublin Trio finished this true story from eleven hundred years ago and pondered the extra-sensory experience animals have in their relationship to people. God made people responsible for Mother Earth and gave them help from God's universe and animals to assist in their causes.

Abraham's Walking Stick

Recently, to everybody's surprise, a large collection of crystals was discovered in Israel. It was spacious in this cavern, which dated to four thousand years ago. It was apparent that the pioneer biblical walkers of the past had visited it. It had a wedding altar where people gathered to get married. Still, to many people's surprise, the most significant discovery in the cavern was the excavation of a walking stick belonging to Prophet Abraham from the Old Testament.

This was a massive discovery of considerable proportions. Considering Abraham's impact on humanity from when God talked to him, he is a pivotal figure from the Old Testament. And the fact that his walking stick was in this cavern was big news, but here's the sad part of it all: Poachers looking to gain a profit found the walking stick, and it was reported to be on the open market. The excavators wanted the walking stick back.

The cavern with the crystals offered a glimpse of underground wonders, with an astonishing freshwater creek with the purest minerals and electrolytes running through the center of the cavern.

It was speculated that the people of Abraham's time used the creek for purification purposes. The organizers of the cavern's discovery hired the Dublin Trio to find the poachers and bring back the walking stick so it could be entered into public review in all its glory.

The Dublin Trio's history was that he was a well-decorated former Green Beret who had dedicated his life to God. The Trio in his name represented the Holy Trinity, which reflected his beliefs. He used a mixture of his discipline as a Green Beret and street smarts and toughness. He was known to get results and spoke several languages. Ryan Shamus was his real name. So, the Dublin Trio traveled to Israel to investigate the disappearance of Abraham's walking stick.

When the Dublin Trio arrived at the crystal cavern, he started looking inside for clues. He was in awe of all the different shapes and sizes of crystals in this cave that formed over thousands of years, but he realized he was there for a mission and continued his investigation. He searched the cavern, including the moisture alongside some of the stones where there was some mud. Lo and behold, there was an impression made by someone's ring. He assumed it was left by one of the poachers as they picked up the walking stick.

He gathered the materials to make a cast of the impression and have a more decisive image to investigate. Once he had that in his possession with distinct markings to work with, the ring led him to a college in Saudi Arabia. When he arrived at the college, his special forces government ID helped him talk to the administrative staff about getting access to the graduation class, which was about thirty people.

He looked into their backgrounds and isolated one person with legal problems with poaching. He identified the person's name and address and proceeded from that point. The Dublin Trio realized the address of this potential prophet was along the same path where Jesus was buried and was in the Christian quarter of the old city of Jerusalem. Being a man of God, he wasn't going to pass up this opportunity to worship his beliefs, because his faith propelled him.

The Dublin Trio arrived, and at the burial place of Jesus, he performed his respectful reflection and contemplation with a high reverence of worship. Although capturing this poacher was important, he only got the opportunity to come to Israel occasionally. He had always pondered the prophet Daniel's account of the fall of Babylon, and since he was on a journey of higher truth, he had heard of corroborating accounts as stated in the Old Testament and sought them out. This included the Babylonian Chronicles, a Babylonian text providing details about the final years of the Nabonidus reign during the fall of Babylon to Cyrus, which aligned with the Book of Daniel's description.

The Book of Daniel mentioned King Belshazzar, and the Babylonian records corroborated this. The Dublin Trio was satisfied that he'd pursued these corroborating chronicles and texts. Many people say that the Old Testament reads like a history book with a lot of dates that reflects the times and advancements during eras in Israel. Events such as the cavern's excavation were starting to support much history from the Old Testament.

Now, the Dublin Trio was ready to pursue these poachers with renewed faith, because the ultimate truth propelled him to hold these criminals accountable. He was seeking justice, so he was on his way to the poacher's address that he'd collected from the college.

He found the poacher's house, and to his surprise, the poacher was with a woman. The moon hung low, casting silvery beams through the partially open window. Clad in dark clothes, the Dublin Trio slipped inside with grace only a trained fighter could muster.

"Did you hear that?" one of the people in bed, a burly man with a scruffy beard, whispered.

"Maybe it's just the wind," his partner murmured, a wiry woman with a fierce glint in her eyes.

"Or it's our uninvited guest," the Trio said, stepping into the moonlight.

"Who the hell are you?" the man roared, springing from the bed.

"Just a friendly visitor," the Trio replied, a smirk on his lips.

The woman lunged first, her fist slicing through the air with a sharp whoosh. The Trio dodged, pivoting smoothly. "Is that the best you've got?"

"Shut up!" she shouted, attempting a roundhouse kick.

He ducked, his foot sweeping low to trip her. "Too slow!"

The man charged, fists swinging wildly, but the Trio was a blur, deflecting blows and weaving through attacks.

"Why are you even here?" the woman gasped, recovering her stance.

"To take you both down," he said, landing a swift kick that sent the man sprawling.

"Guess that's my cue," she grunted, determination igniting in her eyes.

But the Dublin Trio was already there, a dance of precision and strength, and soon, the battle ended with a victorious grin. "I'm here to hold you accountable for stealing the walking stick of Abraham." With the man and woman sprawled out on the floor, the Dublin Trio grabbed Abraham's walking stick to return it to its rightful owner.

The Dublin Trio reflected on the events in this crime. When you worked hard and applied faith to your daily life, anything could happen.

Galactic Battle of the Universe

The Dublin Trio was enjoying sailing on his twenty-five-foot sailboat in the Atlantic off the coast of New England's Cape Cod. Suddenly, he got a mayday from another family in distress on their nearby boat, so he cruised over and saw the boat was sinking. He had to act swiftly. The family's boat got into trouble off the cliffs, where there were lots of rocks. It looked like the family's boat was up against the rocks, causing it to sink.

This was a complex problem for the Dublin Trio because he couldn't navigate his boat with all the large rocks. So, he had to set anchor at a distance and swim to the family's sinking boat. The Dublin Trio jumped into the turbulent waters and set out toward the distressed family. He navigated the rocks and the surf with his expert swimming abilities.

Finally, he reached the sinking boat and helped the family into their life jackets. He had to convince the father to abandon his boat because the father was convinced he could save it. The father reluctantly agreed to surrender the boat. He put on a life jacket and jumped in the water with his family, taking the transmitters with them so they could transmit an urgent signal for help.

The *USS Thomas Jefferson* aircraft carrier picked up their distress call. They dispatched an emergency helicopter to find them. The Dublin Trio stayed with the family until the helicopter detected them. They used their emergency apparatus to bring everybody on board to safety. It wasn't long before the helicopter landed back on board the *USS Thomas Jefferson.*

The Dublin Trio, a ranking former Green Beret with credentials from his past military career, sought out the captain to identify himself. Once those formalities were over, everybody was escorted to their cabins for a good night's sleep. The next morning, the Dublin Trio was awakened to the emergency sound of battle stations, which alarmed him. He immediately grabbed an officer going by his cabin and asked for an update.

The officer said, "I don't know. The instruments on the bridge are going crazy, and we can't figure out why."

The Dublin Trio made his way to the bridge, and the captain allowed him to enter. The Trio saw all the controls going crazy, unable to get a handle on anything. The weather condition panels were stuttering, and the radar was spasming. This was definitely an emergency situation for an aircraft carrier when they couldn't get any kind of read on anything.

Then, suddenly, the weather conditions in front of the aircraft carrier looked ominous as the sky turned dark with green overtones. It unleashed quarter-size hail onto the deck as lightning picked up ferociously in front of the craft. The officers on the bridge witnessed these incredible weather conditions with enlightenment. Then, to their astonishment, a horizontal vortex opened up in front of them, which they could not avoid since it was directly in their path.

The captain yelled with urgency, "All stop! All stop!" But the aircraft carrier could not stop its momentum and got drawn in to the vortex, picking up momentum until it was inside. As they sailed through the vortex, the officers on the bridge noticed they were moving at a high velocity with stars and galaxies passing by them. The experience mesmerized them.

Finally, they stopped deep in space. Somehow, they could go about their business and walk around on the carrier under the protection of a sphere around them. The captain went to his quarters to think about what had just happened, hash it out in his mind, and contemplate his next move, because he was responsible for five thousand people.

While the captain was in his quarters, a spirit appeared before him, the luminous figure of a woman. This spirit spoke to the captain. She said she was the spirit of Joan of Arc and told the captain she was sent to tell him he had a great responsibility. He had been given a great honor by God to defeat an evil army and help restore Godly principles in the universe.

"I am the spirit of Joan of Arc, and I have been in many battles myself. I can help guide you to victory.

Please assemble your officers, and I will address all of you on your mission details together."

The captain, aware that he was just visited by one of God's spirits, was in awe. He tried to gather himself, being responsible for the mighty aircraft carrier with five thousand personnel. He composed his thoughts and prayed to God for guidance in his own private way, and then he gathered all his officers. He also invited the Dublin Trio because of his credentials. Then, he let them all know that "a great responsibility has been given to us."

The luminous, womanly spirit emerged and spoke to the captain and officers. She said, "Satan and his army have rooted themselves on the moon of Vector which is near the star system of Alpha Centauri. It is your mission to seek out and destroy Satan's army base. But before that, there is a bigger problem that needs to be addressed. Satan has created an evil sun that resonates with his evilness, and it is dampening God's values in the universe. God wants you to use your creativity, because he relies on his kingdom with his blessings to work in his honor.

"Once you figure that out, you will then turn your attention to Satan's evil base with his army and armament of fighter jets. God has made subtle adjustments to your instruments so you can operate in interstellar space. For instance, your radar system has been updated to navigate space. In addition, God has put a sphere around your aircraft carrier so the crew can move around in harmony without the effect of gravitational pull. You and your staff must put your heads together and know how to use your nuclear energy in parallel for propulsion in interstellar space.

Good luck, and may the blessings of God and the Kingdom be with you. I'll be watching from a distance."

The captain put his two best machinists on the nuclear energy project, finding a way to parallel this energy into nuclear propulsion, and preparing the aircraft carrier for light-speed capabilities and maneuverability in interstellar space. So, the machinists went to work. The first thing they had to do was to release the huge propellers attached to the carrier. Then, they had to figure out how to transfer the energy.

They delved deeply into the mechanics of nuclear energy and realized that they had to apply temporal mechanics to their theory so the aircraft carrier could use warp fields to create subspace speed technology powered by matter/antimatter reactions to allow them to travel at lightspeed. The machinists released the propellers into space and did their job. The captain was happy to hear they succeeded.

The Dublin Trio was walking down a corridor and overheard two sailors talking about how they were going to sabotage the ship's nuclear propulsion system. Beneath the hum of the engines and the distant clatter of sailors at work, the sinister conversation unfolded near the aft of the ship. "The propulsion system is beyond these doors. Let's knock out the guard and sabotage it."

The Dublin Trio felt a jolt of adrenaline. He'd been trained to handle threats, but this was different. He stepped closer, the shadows cloaking him like a shroud. "Planning something, are we?" he asked, his voice steady, yet laced with authority.

The two sailors turned, surprise flickering across their faces. "What's it to you?" the first one sneered, crossing his arms defiantly.

"I heard you. You need to rethink your choices. I won't let you destroy this ship."

The second sailor laughed, a harsh sound that echoed off the metal walls. "And what are you going to do about it? You think you can take us both? You're outnumbered."

A cold smile crept across the Trio's face. "I've handled worse odds."

Before they could react, he lunged forward, a flurry of movement. The first sailor swung a fist, but the Trio ducked, countering with a precise kick that sent the man sprawling against the steel bulkhead with a grunted, "Oof!"

The second sailor rushed in, fists flying. "You think you're tough? Hah!"

The Trio sidestepped, grabbing the man's arm and twisting it behind his back. He bent low, whispering, "Let's see how tough you are."

"Get off me, you—" The sailor's protest turned into a pained groan as the Trio tightened his grip.

With a swift move, he pivoted, using the sailor's momentum to slam him into the ground. "Stay down," he warned, eyeing the other man regaining his footing.

The first sailor staggered up, rage fueling him. "You're gonna pay for that!"

He charged, but the Trio was already moving, anticipating the blow. "Not today," he murmured, stepping aside and delivering a sharp elbow to the sailor's gut. The man doubled over, gasping.

Breathing heavily, the Dublin Trio turned to the two men sprawled on the cold deck. He had fought in darker places and faced much worse than these two. "Now, how about we call security?"

"Wait—" the first sailor wheezed, panic creeping into his voice.

"No more waiting," the Trio interrupted, pulling out their radio. "This is the Dublin Trio. I need security at the aft immediately. Two sailors attempting sabotage. I've restrained them."

As he waited, the adrenaline ebbed, leaving a sharp clarity in its wake. He glanced at the two men; fear was now etched across their faces. "Maybe next time, choose your battles wisely," he said, the corners of his mouth twitching into a smirk.

The sound of approaching boots echoed through the corridor, a welcome relief. The Dublin Trio stood tall, embodying the weight of his experience, ready to face whatever came next, even if it was just a long day of paperwork the captain required.

The captain decided to recognize the Dublin Trio for his heroism and reestablish his rank as lieutenant from the special OPS unit of the Green Beret Unit. He also put him in charge of one of the platoon units that would be part of the ground invasion when they attacked the evil moon of Vector.

The captain started on his quest to use his imagination and creativity to help God reset the values of the universe. He listed five impactful authors of twenty-first century New Age spirituality: Deepak Chopra, Master Choa Kok Sui, Dr. Caroline Myss, Dr. Wayne Dyer, and Ted Andrews. The captain planned to bring the summation and qualities of each author to the altar in the ship's Church.

Deepak Chopra
Deepak Chopra is known for blending scientific principles with spiritual practices to promote holistic well-being. He emphasizes mind-body connection, integrative medicine, and personal transformation, advocating for practices like meditation, mindfulness, and self-awareness to achieve a state of inner peace and fulfillment.

Master Choa Kok Sui
A former guru of the Pranic Healing Institute and a modern spiritual teacher, he dedicated his life to studying how energy affects overall well-being. He teaches that our primary goal is to improve our state of well-being, not just for ourselves but also for those around us. He emphasizes that we are the sum of our thoughts, actions, and decisions. Since our thoughts shape our experiences, it is essential to be mindful of them, as they influence our lives and our surroundings.

Dr. Caroline Myss

She is well-known in energy medicine, human consciousness, and holistic healing. Her work as a medical intuitive, author, and speaker advocates for a deeper understanding of the connection between our emotional, psychological, and spiritual well-being and physical health. Her key qualities include a strong belief in the power of intuition and the human body's ability to heal and a commitment to exploring the subtle forces that influence our health.

Dr. Wayne Dyer
Dr. Wayne Dyer was a renowned self-help author, speaker, and motivational coach, known for his positive psychology and spiritual teachings. He emphasized the importance of aligning with one's "highest self" and living a life of meaning and purpose, rather than being driven solely by ambition or ego. His work focused on empowering individuals to overcome challenges, develop self-awareness, and manifest desires through conscious choice and intention.

Ted Andrews
Ted Andrews was a highly acclaimed author, teacher, and mystic known for his work in holistic healing. He was a skilled storyteller and speaker, popular in seminars and teaching. Andrews combined his spiritual expertise with practical skills, including music therapy, herbology, and healing modalities like acupressure. He was a talented musician and a certified spiritualist medium.

Meanwhile, the captain received a notification from the bridge as the aircraft carrier came out of light speed and entered orbit around the evil sun. The captain went up to the bridge to assess the situation. The evil sun was invisible, so it couldn't be detected, but the resonance of its rays was dampening the universe with evilness.

The captain sent out a probe with filters so he could capture the natural elements of the universe, like hydrogen, nitrogen, plasma, and atoms. In the meantime, he conferred with his science officer about how to create an etheric natural bomb with a hydrogen armament so when it detonated, it would generate an explosion of natural energy to help disintegrate and break apart the sun's evil resonation because nature was a natural deterrent to evil.

The probe caught enough concentrated natural energy for five hydrogen etheric bombs, which should have a devastating impact on the evil sun. Next, each bomb was designed with evil detection so it could home in on the evil energy resonance of the sun. The science officer worked with his team to develop guidance systems to detect the origin of the evil energy and detonate within its core.

In the meantime, Satan had detected the aircraft carrier in the evil sun's orbit and decided to use the evil sun's defense mechanisms against the carrier. Suddenly, a lethal laser beam came from the sun, but the carrier was ready. They deployed defensive decoys to distract and alter the path of the evil laser beam. A massive explosion off the starboard bow rocked the craft, but the carrier was still intact.

Now was the time for the captain to react. With urgency in his voice, while gripping the stabilizing bar in the bridge, he commanded, "Return fire."

With that order, the carrier released all five hydrogen bombs toward the evil sun. All the crew on the bridge waited with anticipation as they watched the bombs detonate. With the explosion, the evil sun became solid, and they could see the impact of the hydrogen bombs' etheric power. The sun imploded from inside and suddenly vaporized.

There was much jubilee and celebration on the bridge of the aircraft carrier, but there was also something strange out in space. It was dark and semi-transparent, but it had a tangible figure, and it looked like a very large winged angel.

Then, it spoke. "I am the Prince of Darkness. Do you think your manmade weapons are any match for me? How dare you blow up my sun? I will corrupt the thoughts of all those responsible for all the days of your living."

The Dublin Trio stepped forward in the bridge and said, "We are soldiers dedicated to the search for truth, because we believe that all efforts in this cause will redeem us through our faith in God."

Suddenly, a prominent, luminous, womanly figure emerged off the starboard bow separating them from the dark, massive winged angel and spoke to Satan. "I am the spirit of Joan of Arc. I'm here to protect this aircraft carrier, and I carry with me the authority of God. I advise you to leave in peace, or you will upset me and God."

Satan, grudgingly aware that God had the highest power in the universe, reluctantly flew off to strengthen his base on Vector because he anticipated an attack there.

The crew on the bridge said their prayers with gratitude to God and the spirit of Joan of Arc for their protection as they prepared for an aerial attack and ground invasion on the moon, a vector that happened to be in the same solar system. The carrier would be there in a short while, and preparations needed to be made. Meetings with pilots had to occur, and the ground Army platoon meetings would happen to plan a ground invasion.

The aircraft carrier came into orbit around the moon of Vector, and the objective was to blow up Satan's command post on the ground and deal a lethal blow to his aerial combat units.

The *USS Thomas Jefferson* floated in the void of space, a metal leviathan against a backdrop of swirling stars and the ominous glow of the evil moon, Vector. The air buzzed with adrenaline as crew members scurried about, prepping for the mission that could determine the universe's fate.

"Launch sequence initiated!" a voice crackled over the intercom, cutting through the low thrum of the carrier's engines.

"Final checks on the B-2s!" a technician called out, sweat beading his brow.

"Ready to roll, Skipper!" came a response, tinged with excitement and fear.

The F-18 pilots were strapped into their cockpits, hearts racing as they awaited the green light. "Hold onto your helmets, folks," whispered one pilot, his voice barely audible through the comms. "We're about to tango with the devil."

With a lurch, the first wave of stealth bombers and fighter jets shot from the carrier's deck, engines roaring like thunder—VROOOM! They sliced through the darkness, a flock of predatory birds hunting their prey. The B-2s, cloaked in darkness, began their dive toward Vector.

"Target acquired," a pilot murmured, fingers trembling over the controls. "I see them..."

"Engage!" another shouted, a wild laugh escaping him as he released a volley of missiles that streaked through the void like shooting stars.

Explosions lit up the darkness, fiery blooms of orange and red against the black canvas of space. The air crackled with urgency.

"Direct hit! We've got one!" a voice exclaimed, punctuated by triumphant laughter. But the euphoria was short-lived. A volley of enemy fire erupted from the depths of Vector. The air was filled with screams, the sudden silence of a pilot cut short by a burst of enemy fire—BAM!

"Mayday! Mayday!" The frantic voice echoed through the comms, swallowed by static.

"Stay focused! We can't let them take us down!" another pilot shouted, determination lacing every word.

The F18s danced through the chaos, dodging incoming fire with sharp maneuvers, the carriers' crew holding their breath as they watched the screens flicker with data.

"Two bogeys at eleven o'clock!" one of the pilots yelled. "I'm on 'em!"

"Watch your six!" a voice warned, but it was too late. An enemy fighter swooped down, unleashing a barrage of bullets. "Gah! I'm hit!" The cry shattered the comms, followed by a desperate moan.

"Get out of there!" came the urgent reply, but the transmission faded into static.

The tide began to turn. The B-2s and F-18s worked in tandem, exploiting the weaknesses in Satan's aerial defenses. One by one, enemy fighters fell from the sky, their destruction echoing like a twisted symphony of war.

"Push forward! They're breaking!" a pilot shouted, adrenaline surging. With renewed fervor, the American pilots surged ahead, pushing into the heart of enemy territory. The cockpit lights flickered as they unleashed everything they had left.

"Victory is in sight! Let's finish this!" another yelled. As the final enemy fighters retreated into the shadows of Vector, the crew erupted into cheers.

"Mission accomplished! We did it!" The *USS Thomas Jefferson* stood proud, a beacon of resilience amid the cosmic darkness. The universe's fate had shifted, and the light triumphed over the shadows for now.

The Dublin Trio radioed the captain to let him know his platoon had successfully secured Satan's compound, completing the ground invasion. The compound was in U.S. custody, and the entire crew on the *USS Thomas Jefferson* aircraft carrier was in total jubilation with their victories over the evil sun and the evil moon Vector.

Now, the captain had to perform a solemn duty and attempt to reset the values of the universe. He remembered the spirit of Joan of Arc mentioning that it was important for him to be creative while glorifying God. So, the captain took the summation of each of the five spirituality authors to the altar with his officers and said this prayer.

"Supreme Holy God, I come before you with my officers with the summations and the qualities of these five impactful authors of the twenty-first century. I would like to place them on the base of the altar for you to see these qualities. I'm asking you to reset the universe in your lovely divine name and let that power flourish throughout all your creation."

Suddenly, there was a brief illumination of light that expanded beyond what their eyes could see, then the spirit of Joan of Arc spoke to them again. "God was pleased with your triumph over evil, and he has blessed the universe with your authors' values. For a new dawn of hope has arrived for generations to come, and he will help guide you home."

The Dublin Trio was gathering his thoughts as the carrier was guided home to the Atlantic Ocean. He considered how, throughout time and the centuries of man, truth had always come to the surface in its own time. Ultimately, the truth surfaced because he felt truth had its own math, physics, and laws, as its origin is rooted in divine theory. He felt the truth could sometimes be restrictive, depending on the situation at hand, but it always seemed to find its way home.

The Origins of Mankind

A 12-year-old boy came home from playing in the park and showed his father, an archaeologist, two fossils he found off the beaten path on an embankment while he was playing. Because of the nature of his profession, the father was perplexed and interested that these fossils came from a local nearby park. He asked his son exactly where he found the fossils, and his son told him. His dad wanted to see for himself whether there were any other fossils in the area.

Once he arrived, the father investigated the area, and he did find another fossil like those his son found, with ancient, primitive insects on them. The archaeologist then spotted a clearing. He went through the brush and noticed many boulders piled beyond it, so he continued to investigate. He started to climb the boulders, but he jostled one loose and fell, though he was unhurt.

However, the loosened boulder opened an entryway to an ancient cave. Since the father had worn his archaeology outfit, he brought a flashlight, and proceeded into the cave. It was very old, likely dating to the Stone Age. He found more fossils, which compelled him to go deeper into the cave.

Then, he came upon a body of water, which was pretty perplexing. Because he was on a mission of discovery, he had his water testing kit with him. He took samples of the pond of water and waited a few minutes for the results. Shockingly, they came back revealing this pond of water had the beginnings of life in it, with important ingredients such as, amino acids and phosphate compounds. The sampling revealed the water was suitable for these molecules to interact and self-assemble, and with the possible help of other minerals, it could promote life.

This was an incredible find of grand proportions to the archaeologist. Still, he wanted to see what else was in the cave, so he proceeded forward. But he then noticed the ground was suddenly sinking beneath him, and he couldn't escape. It was like quicksand, but it didn't look like quicksand.

He sank quickly, and before he knew it, he passed through and was on the other side, but was in another world. He looked around at the atmosphere, plant life, and ecosystems. From his visual perspective, he suspected he had ventured back in time to the Devonian period, about 359 to 385 million years ago.

He ventured down a nearby path, a road of clues to uncover with wonder and intrigue. He noticed the air was rich with sulfur and nitrogen, making it very pure compared to the atmosphere of modern times. He decided to take out his water testing kit and test the ecosystem of the water from a nearby pond. He found building blocks like phosphorus, nitrogen, and other nutrients fundamental for DNA and other biological processes. The archaeologist tried assembling all the pieces and figuring out their meaning.

In the meantime, after he had been missing for forty-eight hours now, the archaeologist's wife sought out the local authorities and hired the Dublin Trio to look for her husband. The only clue he left was his hat, which remained behind as he sank through the quicksand.

The local authorities didn't want to send anybody through the quicksand after the archaeologist because too much risk was involved, but risk was part of the Dublin Trio's job. He retrieved some rope, tied a ten-pound weight to the end, and threw it into the quicksand in order to create a visible way home after he went through.

The Dublin Trio promised the anthropologist's wife that he would find her husband and bring him back safely, he then went into the quicksand, not knowing his fate. He passed through it and found himself in another world that was far different than the one he came from. Nevertheless, he had a job to do.

He noticed footprints in the path before him. He followed them deeper into the primitive world, and they led him to a cave. The Trio assumed the doctor was in there, so he called out his name several times. To his surprise, the archaeologist came walking out of the cave, puzzled. The Dublin Trio introduced himself to disarm the situation, and the Trio explained that his wife hired them to bring him back to his old reality.

Suddenly, they heard a woman's cry not too far off in the distance. They were astonished because they were under the assumption this period was the beginning and creation of Earth, and they thought nobody was here except themselves. Nevertheless, they were hearing a woman cry out for help.

They followed the sound of the pleas, which led them to a river, where the cries for help got louder. They saw a woman pinned against a big boulder in her canoe. She couldn't get loose, and she was in distress with the mighty current pinning her against the big boulder. Quickly, the Dublin Trio reached down to her. She grabbed his hand, and he hoisted her up to safety as the canoe separated from her. She was exhausted and full of gratitude.

The three of them found shelter nearby, and the professor asked the canoer, "Where did you come from?"

The woman went on to explain that she was a very experienced canoer, and she routinely took groups out for guided tours and weekend tours. She explained that she had been in this strange, primitive world for about a month, using the survival skills she knows. She had gone off a waterfall in a river in their world. She became submerged at the base of the cliff, and when she came up, she looked around and realized she was in a strange new primitive world. She'd been trying to find a way to get back to the world she came from ever since.

The doctor with a PhD in archaeology said they were in an era on Earth where life was just beginning, with single-cell organisms existing in extreme environments. Now, the attention returned to how they would get home. The Dublin Trio reminded everybody that he left a rope behind when he went through the quicksand, and that was their ticket home. They had to climb the rope to return to the old world, so all they have to do was follow the footprints.

As they followed the tracks back toward home, they again crossed the pond where the archaeologist first came across. The doctor explained to them that this pond was rich in phosphorus and other nutrients. Then, awesomely, they saw a bony, ray-finned fish emerge from the pond and use its body to maneuver and navigate the surface. The three of them were in shock to see this extraordinary event, for they were witnessing for the first time that life first came out of a body of natural fresh water.

The archaeologist wanted to take a closer look at the fish. He captured it briefly to examine it and noticed that its gills had a design for respiration. The archaeologist was amazed as he tossed the fish back into the pond. Despite this incredible event, the three of them realized they had to get back home. They followed the footprints, and sure enough, they found the rope which the Dublin Trio had left behind.

The first person up the road was the archaeologist, and as he emerged from the quicksand, the authorities helped him enter his reality, into the loving arms of his wife and son. Then, the expert canoer was next. She went up the rope and returned to her reality. The Dublin Trio felt gratified that he had done his job while also being astonished at the events that took place in this world. He glanced back at the ancient creation where it all began, and then grabbed the rope and returned to his reality as well.

Now on solid ground, the Dublin Trio enjoyed seeing the loving connection of the wife's desire to bring back her husband Then the three of them, the canoer, the archaeologist, and the Dublin Trio, found each other in a group hug of gratitude and friendship stemming from surviving such an incredible event.

They recognized that when you were met with the worst conditions, you must always believe and never give up, because this investment of energy would always give you the best dividends.

The Pastor Vs the Fallen Angel

There was a little boy named Noah, he was 12 years-old, in sixth grade, and had a learning disability that affected his concentration. He would often daydream a lot during class time, and his homeroom teacher would get extremely mad at him and yell at him constantly. The teacher would punish him by taking his index finger and pressing it as hard as he could against the desk, until it almost felt like the finger would snap off. He was a very mean teacher.

However, Noah was very clairvoyant and had a gift from above. One night, while dreaming, he was inspired by an algebraic formula that he wrote down immediately in his notebook. Noah had a gift with math for his age.

The next day in school, the mean teacher was not in, and there was a substitute teacher with a degree in math. When she was walking down the classroom aisle, she saw Noah's algebraic formula that he had written down from his dream. Right away, she recognized the uniqueness and complexity of the formula and asked Noah where he got it.

Noah replied that he received the formula in a dream, so the teacher wrote it down for further study. Once the school day was over, the teacher wrote the algebraic formula on the chalkboard to take a closer look at it. She thought it was different from most formulas she had seen, with a square root expression along with a trigonometric function that was very complicated.

She tried to understand the algebraic formula, the reasoning and thinking, including identifying patterns and looking at symbols to solve the formula. However, the teacher could not understand it all and decided to reach out to her professor at her old college to help her.

Noah's father was a pastor in a Lutheran Church in their hometown of Chicago. He was a former Chicago police officer who retired early to follow his calling to God's ministry at the age of 45, and he wanted to talk to this teacher of Noah's because he was tired of his meanness toward his son.

So, the pastor went out to the teacher's house to speak with him and knocked on the door, but no one appeared to be home. The pastor yelled in through the window, and still no response, so he opened the door and yelled through it. No one answered. The pastor took a risk and went into the house to look around. Nearby, there was a book called *The Fallen Angel Book*. The pastor thought, "What in God's name is this?" He looked at the contents, realizing he didn't have much time, and saw the title, *How to conduct your evilness*, which caught his attention. So, he read the essence of the chapter.

"You must fit into your community and the fabric of your neighborhood and act as normally as possible. Join the PTA, assimilate into the working class of your district, and win the approval of others. This will help you perpetrate your evil more effectively."

The pastor was shocked and wasn't sure what a fallen angel was, but it sounded evil. He went home with this knowledge and Googled "fallen angels" in his browser. The top result was a book by Clair Prophet, who wrote many books, one of which was about fallen angels. The Pastor ordered the book, and while he was waiting for it, he decided to hire someone to protect Noah. After a careful search, he hired The Dublin Trio, a former Green Beret who was proud of his faith and his love of God and was perfect for the job.

The Dublin Trio arrived in Chicago for his new duty of protecting Noah and met with the pastor to discuss his role. The pastor and the Trio sat down, and the pastor explained that Noah is very clairvoyant and sensitive, but had a learning disability. He has had the same teacher since first grade, and the pastor felt his teacher had been very mean to him and contributed to his lack of confidence over the years.

"I believe the teacher is a fallen angel, which greatly concerns me. Based on what I read, these fallen angels do Satan's bidding here on earth. They are spread all over the fabric of our communities at all levels of our country," the pastor explained. "Let me confront this fallen angel, and I'm asking you to protect Noah and help restore his confidence."

As a man of faith, the Dublin Trio understood the situation and his job and wished the pastor well in his conquest.

In the meantime, the substitute teacher went to her former college in the suburbs of Chicago at Northwestern University with the algebraic formula from Noah and visited her quantum physics professor. The professor looked at the formula, realized its distinctiveness and its unique mathematical characteristics. He went to the chalkboard with the formula and tried to make sense of it.

He started making his deductions and trying to solve the equation by finding the value of the unknown variables. To his best astonishing revelation, he believed this algebraic formula that came to Noah in a dream originated from the Big Bang, thirty-six billion years ago. After understanding the magnitude of the moment, the professor collapsed into his chair, and the substitute teacher stood there asking, "What does this mean? Are you okay?"

The professor said, "Do you have any idea what this means? This formula originated from creation thirty-six billion years ago, and this young boy received it in a dream." The professor told the substitute teacher that he would share the formula with eight other esteemed mathematics professors in a group meeting to reveal the uniqueness of this equation.

Over the next few weeks, the professor rounded up the other professors. He wrote Noah's formula on a chalkboard before them, but also had handouts for each of them. He was prepared to present his thesis that the formula originated thirty-six billion years ago.

After the eight professors analyzed the formula, they all agreed that the formula is amazingly unique and deserved to be published with their findings.

In the meantime, the pastor prepared for a showdown with his son's teacher, the fallen angel. To help him in the conflict, the pastor had a special crucifix made of a particular olive wood, which was a religious artifact associated with the Holy Land and carried a symbolic significance within the Christian tradition.

Olive wood was revered as a symbol of peace, prosperity, and fertility. It was said this olive wood came from the Garden of Gethsemane, where Jesus prayed the night before he was captured, and many feel that the wood was highly blessed.

The pastor, empowered with his blessed crucifix, was now ready to face the fallen angel. He braced for the unknown because he was unaware of the depths and access this teacher had to the dark side.

He arrived at the teacher's house to confront him. He knocked on the door, and the teacher answered. At first, their conversation was cordial because the teacher was unaware the pastor knew he was a fallen angel, and the angel was very clever and devious. He would do anything to keep up the illusion that he was normal and lived an everyday life.

But the pastor knew better after studying the lives of fallen angels. He interrupted the teacher in mid-conversation and said, "Don't pull this crap with me, I know who you are, and if you have a problem with my son, then you have a problem with me."

The teacher replied, "The problem is that your son holds back the curriculum in the class and needs to be punished for that"

"Your cruelty is born from the dark side, because you're a fallen angel and I'm here to confront you," the pastor said.

"Don't make me laugh," the teacher said. "You have no idea the depths to which I can torture you, pastor."

"I have full confidence in the glory of my faith and God that the principles of God's providence will prevail over you."

Then, suddenly, a kitchen chair moved at a high velocity from the dining room through the living room and hit the pastor's knee where he was sitting, which made him fall to the floor in acute pain, holding both hands over the knee. The teacher stood over the pastor, laughing.

But the pastor, not giving up, pulled out his olive wood crucifix, gathered himself, and rose staggeringly to face the teacher. He pointed the crucifix at the teacher and spoke Psalm 23 aloud.

"The Lord is my shepherd, I shall not want. He made me lie down in green pastures and led me beside still waters. He restores my soul, he leadeth me in the paths of righteousness for his name's sake. Yea, though I walk through the valley of the shadow of death, I will fear no evil. For thou art with me, thy rod and thy staff, they comfort me. Thou preparest a table before me in the presence of my enemies, thou anointest my head with oil, my cup runneth over.

Surely goodness and mercy shall follow me all the days of my life, and I will dwell in the House of the Lord forever."

The evil teacher beckoned the darkness of evil to rise against the Pastor, and the logs in the fireplace started rattling. The fallen angel started to laugh at the pastor as an image of the Devil appeared next to the teacher to show solidarity with the teacher, which horrified the pastor.

Still, he stayed disciplined in his cause, resolute with purpose, and said, "May the Kingdom of God rebuke and repel you, for you will understand that God has the ultimate power."

Then, a stream of energy with beautiful, powerful white particles came in through the window, filling and circulating through the room. The image of the Devil disappeared, and the evil atmosphere dissipated. At first, the teacher was confused, but then realized that God had intervened. The teacher wasn't happy with how quickly his understanding of the dark side abandoned him when God showed up.

For now, the Dublin Trio was with Noah, and part of the Trio's responsibility was to help restore Noah's confidence after being with the evil teacher for six years. "Noah, I would like to talk to you about your faith, which is your guiding force for your beliefs and actions and will help you influence everything from decision-making to future relationships. Reading positive content is important because it will always shape your reality. Your brain will respond and help you transcend all good content you read, strengthening you to become a better man. Take my business card, and you can call me anytime you want to talk."

In the interim, the pastor noticed and looked at the teacher's face when the dark energy abandoned him. When God showed up, the pastor saw this as an opportunity to solidify God's will and said, "There is only one true power connected to God's majesty. A power that will never leave you, because God's power will fortify you in many ways. Take my hand and pray with me. We'll launch a new beginning with the power that is eternal."

The teacher agreed. The pastor and the teacher prayed together in unison because, as it has been taught throughout the ages, love is the most powerful energy in the universe.

Dan McMeans

The Dublin Trio's Intervention

The Dublin Trio was on a twenty-five-passenger commuter plane from New York to Philadelphia. While he was enjoying his flight, an urgent issue came up with the flight attendants. All three pilots had become violently ill and could not operate the plane, and the plane was on autopilot, which was a temporary solution. The plane needed a pilot to have dialogue with the tower.

When the flight attendants reflected on what might have happened to the pilots, they recalled a suspicious waitress in the pilot's lounge who they had never seen before. They felt she had something to do with the pilots all becoming ill, and they suspected maybe she poisoned them.

The flight attendants didn't want to alarm everyone about the situation with the ill pilots. They decided to Google the passenger list and check each person's background qualifications to see if they had the mental capabilities to pilot the plane, and they came across Ryan Shamus, The Dublin Trio. They discovered he was a former special ops Green Beret

72

operating as a civilian, helping people in their private lives. They thought he was the man for the job, so they approached him privately and told him the situation.

He went with them to the cockpit and, once behind closed doors, he told them that he never operated a plane before. The flight attendants pleaded with him that he was their only hope based on his background. They also told the Trio that a senator was on board from Delaware, so he should be aware of the situation.

So, the Dublin Trio took command of the commuter plane and started communicating with the tower. The tower started to familiarize the Trio with all the commands on the plane and tried to explain that they would do their best to guide them to a safe landing.

The flight attendants gave a briefing to the senator on board about what was going on. But as they were walking back toward the cockpit, two men emerged from their seats with switchblades they had hidden in their shoes, grabbed one of the flight attendants, and said, "We're taking over this plane and redirecting it to Iran, and we are capturing the senator on board. Now, I want the flight attendants to take us to the cockpit."

As he held a knife to the flight attendant's neck, they went forward to the cockpit, and once they arrived, they started to order the Dublin Trio to open the door or they would kill the flight attendant.

At first, the Dublin Trio was resistant, because he knew the ramifications if he let the terrorists get in the cockpit. He yelled through the cockpit door and told the flight attendants to use whatever force they could to fight off the terrorists. The attendants fought back because they had metal cutlery, so they surprised their intruders with butter knives and forks.

The women put up a good fight, but the terrorists were able to prevail because they were stronger. They yelled to the Trio, directly ordering him to open to cockpit door or they would kill one of the attendants. The Trio didn't want any harm to come to them, so he complied, and the terrorist redirected the plane to Iran.

The plane landed in Iran, and the senator and the Dublin Trio were redirected to a room for briefing. The terrorists laid out their plan to the senator, where they wanted him to be an advocate on behalf of the Iranian government in support of the Iranian nuclear program and a voice in support of moving forward with a peaceful accord with the Iranian government. Then, the verbiage got violent with the senator, threatening him and his family if he did not comply, telling him that they knew where he lived and what school his children went to, and if he did not comply, deadly repercussions would come his way.

They turned to the Dublin Trio and said to him, "That goes for you, too." Then, they hauled the Trio off to a jail cell until a plane was ready to take him and the senator back home.

In the jail cell next to the Dublin Trio was a man who identified himself as a CIA operative the Iranian government had captured. He told the Dublin Trio that the Iranian government was much closer to nuclear capability than they were saying. They were giving the appearance that they were three months away when they were actually two weeks out, and

74

something needed to be done about it immediately. He asked if by any chance, the Trio had a military background.

After their discussion, he concluded the Dublin Trio was their only hope. "You'll have to break free when they leave you and go to the nuclear lab room," the CIA agent said.

The Dublin Trio told the operative that he would come back for him and find a way to set him free.

It wasn't long before the guards came for the Trio to escort him out of the jail cell. They went about a hundred feet down the hallway with two guards flanking him, weapons slung low, their eyes scanning the corridor ahead. "Keep moving," one of them barked, shoving the Trio forward.

He felt the weight of their stares, the tension of their fingers resting lightly on their triggers. He had to act fast. The mission depended on it. With a glance, he assessed the guards. One was stocky, a bear of a man with a thick beard, and the other was wiry, all sharp angles and quick movements. He'd seen men like them before. They were tough, but he had a few tricks up his sleeve.

The Trio's heart raced, not only from fear, but from the thrill of the challenge. He took a deep breath, feeling the adrenaline surge through his veins.

"Why do they keep us down here?" the bearded guard muttered, glancing at his partner.

"Shut it," the wiry one snapped. "Just follow orders."

The Trio seized the moment. He pivoted sharply, catching the wiry guard off balance. A swift kick dove into the guard's midsection, the air whooshing out of him with a pained "Oof!"

Before the bearded guard could react, the Trio dropped low, sweeping his leg out to knock the guard down. A sharp thud echoed as the guard hit the ground, dazed.

"Nice try!" The Trio smirked, snatching the guard's weapon and pivoting to face the remaining threat.

The wiry guard was scrambling to his feet, eyes wide with shock. "You'll pay for that!" he shouted, lunging forward, fists flying.

"You'll have to catch me first," the Trio laughed, dodging the clumsy strike. His body moved with practiced grace, each motion fluid as he ducked and weaved. The wiry guard was fast, but the Trio had the advantage of surprise. He sidestepped, delivering a quick jab to the guard's ribs.

"Ugh!" A grunt escaped the guard's lips as he stumbled back against the wall.

The Trio advanced, weapon raised, "You want to play rough? Let's see how you like this." In one swift motion, he disarmed the guard, twisting the gun from his grip.

The wiry man's eyes widened in disbelief. "Damn it!" he spat, realizing he'd underestimated his opponent.

Now armed, the Trio faced both guards. The bearded one groaned as he regained his senses, pushing himself up from the floor. "Get him!" he roared, shaking off the daze.

The Trio smirked, adrenaline coursing through him. "You think you can take me?" With a sudden burst of energy, he charged forward, flipping the gun in his hand, a dance of chaos unfolding in the dim corridor.

"Stop!" the wiry guard shouted, desperation creeping into his voice, but it was too late—the Trio was already moving, a blur of fists and feet, reclaiming control of his fate. As he subdued the last guard, he felt the moment's weight settle. Time was cheap, but he had no intention of wasting it.

"Now," he muttered, securing the weapons, "let's find that nuclear lab."

With a final glance at the guards, he slipped into the shadows of the hallway, the faint hum of his surroundings fading behind him, replaced by the quickening rhythm of his heart. The stakes were high, but so was his resolve.

The Dublin Trio made his way to the guarded nuclear facility, wearing one of the guard officers' uniforms, so he would have the element of surprise when he arrived. Naturally, after the Dublin Trio and the nuclear facility guard engaged in small talk, the guard realized that the Dublin Trio lacked credentials.

Hence, the Trio quickly positioned himself and swiftly delivered a sidewinder kick, followed by another kick to the midsection, and then an uppercut, which sent the guard reeling to the ground. Then, the Trio had access to the lab, and he went to work.

His objective was to sabotage the nuclear testing for a few weeks until he could get in touch with the U.S. government to let them know the Iranian nuclear capabilities were much further along than what they were telling them. He located eight or nine two-gallon water containers and started filling them up. Once filled, the Trio poured and mixed the water with the lab materials to contaminate them. When the Iranians used them, it would compromise their ability to combine atoms and create nuclear energy.

It was time for the Dublin Trio to go back and free the CIA agent, the flight attendants, the senator, and the pilots who survived their illness, who were all in the same cell block. The plan was for all of them to get out onto the tarmac and grab a plane. The Trio grabbed the keys from the unconscious nuclear lab guard and returned to the cell block. He realized the cell doors were operated by one lever that required a key to operate it, and that was what he did.

The Trio gave one of his weapons to the CIA agent, so they were both armed. They, the senator, the flight attendants, and the pilots snuck out onto the tarmac where the planes were and made a mad dash for the closest available plane. As they were running out, gunfire came from the airport guards. The Trio and the CIA operative returned fire, as the others ran into the plane.

Finally, everybody was on the plane, and the pilots took off, quickly ascending into the airspace. It wouldn't be long before Iran sent up fighter planes to shoot them down, though. The CIA operative got on the radio, contacted the closest aircraft carrier, and identified himself with his security codes. Before they knew it, two F-18 fighter planes were dispatched to protect the plane.

The U.S. fighter planes saw the Iranian planes ready to engage and sent a warning. The Iranian planes withdrew, and they were all heading home safely with important information for the U.S. government.

They felt that they had done their patriotic duty, because we all have to work together in purpose and sacrifice for our great country to continue its liberties like no other country in history.

Indian Chief Massasoit

On September 6,1620, the Mayflower, which had 102 pilgrims on it, made its sixty-six-day voyage across the Atlantic. The ship anchored in Plymouth Meeting on November 11, 1620.

Their quarters were severely cramped during their ocean voyage. They had no private chambers or windows. Most people stayed below decks due to rough seas, and one-third of the passengers were children. They didn't have much food or rations during the voyage.

There wasn't much time before winter would start when they landed, but the pilgrims were good carpenters and built structures for their colony in about three weeks. Nevertheless, the harsh winter and lack of food took the lives of forty percent of the pilgrims during the first winter. If it hadn't been for the collaboration between the Native Americans and the pilgrims, the pilgrims' survival would have looked bleak.

Chief Massasoit was the intertribal chief of all the Wampanoag tribe who inhabited parts of present-day

Massachusetts and Rhode Island, particularly the coastal regions. In March 1621, several months after the landing of the Mayflower at Plymouth, Chief Massasoit journeyed to the colony with his colleague Samoset, who had already made friendly overtures to the pilgrims.

Convinced of the value of thriving trade with the newcomers, Chief Massasoit set plans in motion to ensure peaceful accord between the races. This included the Wampanoag tribe teaching the pilgrims how to till and nurture the land to ensure a healthy harvest so they would survive the following winter and showing them techniques for planting, fishing, and cooking that were essential to survival in the wilderness.

All these things were necessary, but one of the most enduring and endearing traditions that we cherish today as Americans, which is Thanksgiving, wouldn't be possible without the contributions of the pilgrims and Chief Massasoit and the Wampanoag tribe, who came together in peace and harmony to celebrate the union of their peoples.

Someone in Chief Massasoit's ancestral lineage contacted the Dublin Trio, inviting him to their house in Maine for a discussion about lost opportunities on behalf of the Wampanoag tribe. This person happened to be a woman, and she felt the modern celebration of Thanksgiving lacked acknowledgement for the sacrifices of this great Native American chief. She wanted to express her feelings to someone in government authority, namely the Dublin Trio, the ex-Green Beret who still carried government credentials.

When they met, the woman descended from the former great chief discussed her concerns and brought them to the surface. The Dublin Trio, who had a whole new respect for Chief Massasoit, said he would follow through and put it on his website.

The woman invited the Dublin Trio to meditate with her. She asked him to meet her at her meditation place, which was in the central area of the forest, a three-hundred-foot walk from her house. The Dublin Trio decided to take a nice stroll to her meditation place. While he was walking down the dirt path, the sun dipped low behind the trees, and the earthy scent of pine mixed with the crisp air.

He was relishing the tranquility, the leaves whispering secrets, when a sudden rustle shattered the peace. A large black bear emerged from the brush, her cubs trailing close behind. His heart raced. He froze, aware of the gravity of the encounter. The bear eyed him, muscles tense, a low growl rumbling from her throat.

"Easy, girl," he murmured, palms sweating around the hilt of his hunting knife. But the bear didn't relent. With a snarl, she charged, claws glinting as she raced down the path.

"Not going down without a fight," he thought, taking a step forward, his voice steady. "Come on!"

The bear lunged, jaws snapping. He sidestepped, slashing with the knife. The blade found its mark, and the bear roared in pain. The battle raged, a frenzy of fur and fear, until he struck deep with one final thrust. The bear collapsed, silence falling like a shroud.

Panting, the Dublin Trio stepped back, heart hammering. He surveyed the scene, gratitude washing over him as he resumed his path, a warrior among the trees.

He met the woman at her meditation place, and they meditated together. He had much to be thankful for after surviving a brutal bear attack.

After the Dublin Trio returned to his room, he was filled with questions about Chief Massasoit and Googled the history of this great man, who had been unceremoniously not mentioned in association with Thanksgiving. He found a painting that illustrated a genuine Thanksgiving between the pilgrims and the Wampanoag tribe. As he regarded the illustration, he noticed one of the Native Americans was wearing a bandana with an inscription in their language.

The Dublin Trio wrote down the inscription, returned to Chief Massasoit's descendent, and asked her to interpret the words. She told him that it meant "hope," and the Dublin Trio left the woman's house inspired. He was in deep thought about the union during 1623.

As he did more research, he realized Chief Massasoit had worked to ensure a peaceful accord between the races as long as he lived. When the chief became dangerously ill in the winter of 1623, he was nursed back to health by the grateful pilgrims and the colonist leader, Governor Edward Winslow, who was said to have traveled several miles through the snow to deliver nourishing medicine to the chief.

Thanksgiving, as it is today, is an excellent memory of the traditions of families coming together in union, sharing loving bountifulness. It is one of our greatest American virtues. Perhaps when we look back on the union between the Pilgrims and the Wampanoag tribe, our greatest virtue may be knowing that we can respect our differences and maintain tolerance to help promote peace and understanding.

This virtue fueled families across America to celebrate our greatest strength as a nation: our family bonds. Anything is possible from that core.

Journey into the Crater

Ryan Shamus, a former special forces Green Beret with unique skills, embarked on journeys and adventures to further the pursuit of the human spirit because this was his calling from above. His alias was the Dublin Trio, and the Trio in his name represented the Father, the Son, and the Holy Ghost.

The Dublin Trio received an urgent call from the North Island of New Zealand that a twelve-year-old girl had fallen into a vast crater. The authorities said the girl took a significant fall, and they could not see her from the surface. They knew the Dublin Trio had considerable experience in rappelling. The issue was that the girl had fallen three months ago, and her family and authorities were very alarmed.

So, the Dublin Trio arrived in New Zealand to examine the Mahuika Crater for his descent to the bottom, where they believe the girl fell. He learned from the local authorities the scope of the crater in terms of measurements. The diameter of the crater was 1.2 miles, and the depth was two hundred feet, which was alarming because he knew from experience that it was difficult to survive a fall like that unless you landed on a soft surface. He was concerned for this girl's well-being.

The Dublin trio successfully used rappelling techniques to reach the bottom of the crater, but he did not see the little girl. Oddly, he found numerous footprints walking away from the area that led to a passageway beneath the crater. He followed the footprints and entered the passage, which looked ancient. He wasn't sure where he was heading, so he proceeded cautiously.

Then, he saw a message on the wall. It said, "I am Noah Zealander. I traveled down, and I got trapped. This message is to warn you not to go further." But the Dublin Trio was hired to find the girl, though he would take the message from this traveler from the past under consideration.

He ventured forward until he came across hot lava running in a current that blocked his path to get from one side to the other. So, he found a large, uprooted tree at an angle near the bottom of the current. The Dublin Trio climbed the big oak to the top and started swaying the tree to loosen it, hoping to leverage it so would fall across the lava current. He wrestled with this tree, swaying and jostling it until it broke free and slammed down across the lava flow, allowing him to cross.

The Trio proceeded down the eerie passageway until he came to a sudden cliff. The depth beneath him was so dark that he couldn't see the bottom, but he had to cross the chasm to continue his journey looking for this girl, because the footprints stopped there. There were vines available, so he tugged on several of them, testing their sturdiness. He had to make sure he chose the strongest vine to cross the fifty-foot gap.

Finally, he found a sturdy vine and took a perilous leap of faith. He landed safely on the other side of the cliff and continued his journey down into the Earth. The deeper he walked toward the center of the Earth, the more he realized something significant was going on. He started to feel that time was loosening around him. Being a wise man who studied physics, he started to wonder whether the center of the Earth had its own mathematics transcending space and time, like black holes in the universe that contain separate dimensions.

Suddenly, an eight-foot winged bat with six-inch fangs appeared from the shadows and approached the Dublin Trio, which was alarming. The Trio reached for his sword. The Dublin Trio was perplexed, wondering what was going on and how this bat appeared out of thin air.

Then, the air thickened with an eerie chill as the Dublin Trio ventured deeper into the cavern. Shadows danced along the walls, flickering like ghosts in the dim light of his lantern. The Dublin Trio thought he heard something, and his grip tightened around the hilt of his sword. Suddenly, the bat's massive shape unfurled from the darkness. The Trio froze as the creature let out a bone-chilling screech.

The bat approached him and swooped low, its claws glinting, aiming straight for the Dublin Trio. With a swift motion, he raised his sword, the blade gleaming. The bat lunged, but the Trio dodged, delivering a powerful strike.

"Not today!" he shouted, ducking as the creature retaliated with a furious flap that swirled gusts of wind. The Trio growled and spun to counter. As his sword connected with the bat's flank, it let out a pained screech and faltered. With one final blow, the bat retreated into the shadows, leaving only the echo of its screech behind.

The Trio stood breathing heavily, the cavern suddenly silent. *Finally, it's gone*, he said to himself.

The Dublin Trio thought about how and why this giant bat came to be. He remembered feeling like he was slipping into a different time zone. Impossible mystical creatures could use a time portal to manifest. This was worrisome to him. As he considered this, he stumbled over a large amethyst rock. Because he had a background in spirituality with crystals and rocks, he knew amethysts were associated with tranquility and spiritual awareness. He also knew they could elevate one's sense of universal consciousness.

This amethyst was huge, and the Trio didn't want to treat it disrespectfully. He picked it up and contemplated his journey from Green Beret to private contractor, helping people. As he showed gratitude, a monstrous woman appeared with snakes in her hair. The Dublin Trio knew this was Medusa from Greek mythology, which frightened him because he was aware of her ability to turn targets to stone.

He tried to take cover, but it was too late. Medusa's unleashed evil energy turned him to stone.

Medusa, feeling victorious, moved on through the cavern. But something mystical was starting to happen. The Dublin Trio was a man of faith. The amethyst rock he held began to emit energy, dissolving the stone that held the Trio captive and slowly returning him to human form.

Then, before he knew it, the Dublin Trio was his old, intrepid self. The next time he battled with Medusa, he would be ready. He went looking for the right kind of rock to serve as a reflector. After finding such a rock, he began polishing it. To his surprise, Medusa appeared from behind a giant boulder.

The air was tense as she stepped out, her serpentine hair writhing like a nest of vipers. The cavern glowed with an eerie light, reflecting off the Dublin Trio's polished stone. He stood defiantly, his body still taut from their recent struggle.

"Well, well," Medusa hissed, her voice a cold whisper that echoed against the cavern walls. "You escaped. How...unexpected." Her eyes narrowed, dark and dangerous. "You think you can stand against me?"

"Let's find out," said the Dublin Trio, confidence lacing his voice. With a flick of her gaze, she unleashed her deadly stare, a beam of petrifying energy aimed straight at him. He raised the reflective stone high, deflecting her malevolent glare back toward her.

A blinding flash erupted, and Medusa's scream echoed off the walls. "No, no!" The light illuminated her, and she began to freeze, solidifying into the stone she had so often wielded against others.

"Looks like you've been stoned!" the Dublin Trio responded with confidence.

He gathered his belongings and continued down the path where the footprints led. He came to a clearing with a descent where the incline was manageable. From here, he could see a clearing down below with around15 straw huts. This baffled him, because he thought the crater was abandoned.

The Dublin Trio proceeded with caution. As he drew within 150 feet of the huts, the people living in them emerged to greet this visitor from above, because it was a rarity for anyone from the surface to reach this community. Then, the people from the huts divided as one man came up the middle to address the Dublin Trio. The leader of the community said, "State your business."

The Dublin Trio told the leader he had been hired to look for a girl who fell into the crater three months ago, and asked if he knew or had seen her.

The leader said, "We are the Utopian People. The values of our community are to live in a groundswell of ideas that propel us toward a greater goal. Please keep our community a secret. We moved down here hundreds and hundreds of years ago and enjoy our privacy. We have the girl in question. When she fell, she broke her leg, and we helped her mend it so she could walk again. We'll proudly give her back to you so you can return her to her family."

So, the Dublin Trio took the girl, who looked forward to being returned to her family. They followed the same path back to where she fell, and eventually, she was lovingly reunited with her family. The Dublin Trio kept the solemn oath that was asked of him to ensure the community that lived underground remained secret, as they requested.

The Mysterious Fog

The Dublin Trio received a fax for his next assignment to check out a mysterious, malevolent fog haunting ten luxurious homes at a lake called Lake Rejuvenation, an offshoot near the Great Lakes. These homeowners have been complaining that the fog had a sinister, malevolent feel, that it mysteriously came from nowhere, and they were concerned for their well-being. Local authorities didn't seem to care. They saw the Dublin Trio's name on a web page, so they contacted him, and he was off and running to Lake Rejuvenation.

He arrived at the lake, which was beautiful. No one would ever know anything mysterious had happened there. He planned to attend a town meeting with all the homeowners that night to gather more information to help them with their cause.

The Dublin Trio arrived at the homeowners' meeting and heard all their concerns. He started asking questions, but no real revelations came to his attention. While the homeowners were taking a beverage break to relax for a minute or two, one of them approached the Dublin Trio with negative energy. He thought he was superior to other people and wanted to pick their guest's mind.

But the Trio was a highly decorated special forces communicator, skilled and prepared to handle himself in all cases. They engaged in conversation, and the man with bad intentions was looking for angles to exploit while talking. The Dublin Trio noticed this man wearing a peculiar necklace, which he registered in his mind. He exited the conversation and mingled with other people, and when the man in question wasn't looking, he took a picture so he could study the necklace with more clarity when he got home.

Once the Trio returned home, he zoomed in on the necklace with his phone. To his shock, he discovered through the Internet that it was the Devil's Demon of Baphomet necklace, which was evil. The Dublin Trio concluded that this was a clue because the luxury homeowners' main complaint was that this fog was sinister and malevolent. This guy was wearing an evil necklace, and who knew what his intentions or origins were. It was worth pursuing.

Later that night, the Dublin Trio went to the man's house while he was sleeping, in order to gather more proof. He broke through a basement window without shattering the glass and walked around the basement. There, he found an altar for worshipping dark forces, which was uncomfortable to look at.

Still, here it was in real life. On this altar was an old Bible of an evil nature, and the Dublin Trio took it because he needed a deeper understanding of this person's mindset. Then, he exited the house the same way he'd came, without detection, and took the Bible home to look at.

He spent the night reading the disturbing, evil Bible and the things it advocated. It was frightening and disturbing to see, because as the Dublin Trio navigated through the volume, he realized this evil person intended to appear as normal as possible to the general public so he could gain trust to do his evil work. The evil book went on to reinforce that if you were going to work on behalf of the dark forces, you would need to assimilate yourself into the fabric of your community. He found his man, who had to be stopped at all costs.

The Dublin Trio went to the library to try to dig up local records with information that may be helpful to him about the area townsfolk or news from the past, but he couldn't really find anything. However, he did not give up. He sat and thought, and soon recalled that the Native Americans were here well before the English settlers. He looked up folklore in that area and found a highly spiritual Native American chief who had battled with evil spirits during the 1500s.

According to the folklore, the evil spirits were many. They tried to attack the chief, who held a strong belief in nature spirits and sky spirits. He prayed to the spirits, and they helped him capture the evil spirits to teach them a lesson that God protects his people through the elements of nature. The Native American chief was able to gather up the evil spirits attacking him and place them under the lake in captivity, because water was a natural repellent of evil energy.

The Dublin Trio left the library inspired, for he had an idea of what was going on here. He believed the man with the necklace from the town meeting was somehow accessing the evil spirits' capabilities and causing this fog to haunt the homeowners, but why? Realizing he still had the evil Bible, he thought maybe something there would give him a clue as to the man's intentions for perpetrating this sinister fog.

So, the Dublin Trio went home and looked through the volume. He found information that one of the original homeowners had a time capsule placed before the construction of their home five hundred years ago, and in this time capsule was something very valuable to the man in question and his evil worship. According to notes on a piece of paper stuck in the evil Bible, the evil artifact in the time capsule was known to extract more evil power, and if it fell into the wrong hands, it could cultivate wrongdoing.

Now the Trio knew the man's intentions. He wanted to access the time capsule and was trying to scare off the homeowners in order to excavate it himself. It was time to confront the man.

The Dublin Trio went to the man's house and entered. A faint scent of whiskey lingered in the air, mingling with the tension radiating from the man seated at the table with two thugs alongside him.

"Enough games." With a sharp command, the man in question waved a hand. "Boys, show them what happens when you poke the bear!"

The thugs lunged, fists flying. The Dublin Trio instinctively grabbed a nearby two-by-four, swinging it with a crack against one thug's midsection.

"Ugh!" he gasped, doubling over. With a final crack of wood against flesh, both thugs lay groaning. Just then, the man bolted for the door.

Tires screeched as the man fled in his vehicle, adrenaline coursing through him. He couldn't look back, because the Dublin Trio was right on his tail. The Dublin Trio beat his knuckles on the steering wheel as he chased the man through the twisting streets.

"Look out," a woman yelled, ducking as she barely jumped out of the way of the two cars. The evil man swerved and tried to speed down a narrow alley, but the Trio maneuvered his vehicle to cut him off. With a loud thud, both cars came to a halt.

"Get out," yelled the Trio as he yanked the man's car door open. He reached in, grabbed the evil man, and pulled him out of the car with force. He straightened him against the car with a forearm under his throat, tightening his grip. "I'm going to drag you to the town hall meeting, and you're going to confess your intentions, or I'll take my evidence to the police.

The evil man's eyes darted. Realizing he was trapped in the heart of the city, surrounded by limited options, he conceded to the Trio's demands.

The Dublin Trio and the evil man both showed up at the town hall meeting with the other nine homeowners. The evil man started to feel the weight of the guilt upon his shoulders for what he had done as the other homeowners listened with compassion, let him express his guilt, and felt his sincerity and decided to forgive him for his actions. The man was very moved by the homeowners who forgave him and the power of forgiveness. He thought maybe it was time to look at life from a different lens.

The man in question felt better and a little more at peace with himself after clearing the air and releasing negative thoughts. He wanted to explore this meaning more deeply, so all ten homeowners were looking forward to starting a new chapter of moving together in peace, love, and harmony, believing that anyone was worth having faith in when they showed signs of hope and remission.

The Dublin Trio felt gratified that he was part of this process. Looking at it from a bigger picture, he believed when resentment met loving intentions, loving intentions usually won, because that source was inexhaustible.

Torresdale Prison Ghost

The Dublin Trio had a request to investigate from the residents who live alongside Torresdale Prison, constructed in 1896 and closed in 1995. The residents had been claiming for the last few years that they had seen a mysterious, ghost-like figure roaming the grounds of the prison, located in the Holmesburg section of Philadelphia. In particular, they would see this ghost-like figure walking near the outer wall of the prison.

This was a short trip for the Dublin Trio, because he lived in Northeast Philadelphia. He met the residents at one of their homes and started asking questions about this mysterious ghost. Collectively, they didn't have much to say except that he appeared at night when it was dark out, after 10 PM. He seemed to be walking the grounds along the prison wall, which was about 400 yards long and 50 feet high, with guard towers. It was a foreboding presence, standing as a stark reminder in this community of the correction facility that helped rehabilitate prisoners.

One of the residents invited the Dublin Trio to stay with them that night and observe the ghost-like figure, and the Trio accepted. He got comfortable in the guest house with a view of the prison and eagerly waited until 10 PM. At that time, he saw a ghostly, translucent white figure with a human shape floating and walking outside the wall's perimeter.

At first, the Dublin Trio was intrigued and studied the ghost, but suddenly, the figure went through the wall and disappeared. Wanting to pursue him and unravel all the ghost's secrets, the Dublin Trio grabbed his climbing gear and headed to the wall where the ghost had disappeared. He ascended the wall, then rappelled down the other side.

The ghostly figure stood in the courtyard, pointing toward a particular door, and the Dublin Trio felt the ghost was trying to tell him something. He walked up to the door, opened it, and descended the stairway he found beyond it. The old prison loomed as the Dublin Trio cautiously maneuvered down the hallway with its crumbling walls and whispering secrets. A low growl echoed as he moved along the dim corridor, sending a shiver down his spine.

"Sounds like two," the Trio said to himself, fingers tightening around a pipe he had found. Before he could react, a Doberman Pinscher lunged from the darkness, teeth bared and eyes wild. He raised his forearm just in time to divert the dog's vicious bite. The impact jolted him, but he held his ground.

The second dog, a hulking Rottweiler, joined the fray, barking ferociously. The Trio twisted the pipe to block a snap of its jaws. He wrestled with the growling beasts, adrenaline surging through him. The Trio found his footing, pushing back against the Rottweiler's weight.

"Focus!" he shouted, dodging a snap from the Doberman. He sent the Rottweiler sprawling with a final shove, while the Doberman yelped and retreated. Panting, the Trio glanced at the battered beasts, their snarls fading into whimpers. "Let's move before they regroup", he said, shaking off the adrenaline as they pressed deeper into the prison's shadows.

He followed the ghostly figure down the corridor to a cell. The figure pointed to the dirt floor, and the Trio realized the ghost wanted him to dig at this spot, but he needed a shovel. So, he went back out into the corridor and down until he found the landscaping room. He grabbed a shovel, returned to the cell in question, and started to dig.

Soon, the Dublin Trio found a metal crate. He pulled it out of the hole, opened it, and discovered an accounting book and a diary. The Trio was perplexed as to what this meant, so he took the container with these two items back to the resident who let him stay in the guest house. The guest house had a desk that he could use.

Upon reviewing the contents of the accounting book and the diary, he found interesting information about the transfer of the Birdman of Alcatraz. The Dublin Trio was intrigued, so he Googled the term and found out the Birdman's real name was Robert Stroud, who was convicted of murder and sentenced to a life term but rehabilitated himself through his love and understanding of birds.

While serving time at Leavenworth Penitentiary, the man we knew as the Birdman of Alcatraz found a nest in his cell. The bird was injured, and with permission from the guards, he was allowed to care for the bird in the nest. People believed that his love and caring of this bird let him to become a respected ornithologist and the author of *The Ecology of Birds*. With his attention and nurturing for these creatures, he had slowly rehabilitated himself.

However, an awful travesty had occurred. As the Dublin Trio pieced everything together, he realized there was once an assistant who worked for the warden. The assistant uncovered a racketeering program the warden had undertaken, charging an exorbitant fee to the prisoners' girlfriends and wives for private sessions with their boyfriends or husbands in the structures designed to give them privacy. These structures were supposed to be free and provided by the state. Still, this warden charged a small fortune to use them, and he'd been doing it for years. He did not want to see it end.

The assistant who knew about the warden's racketeering program ended up sacrificing his life when the warden had him murdered and buried in that cell. So, the ghostly figure was not malevolent. He wanted his story told so he could rest in peace. The Dublin Trio had all the evidence he needed to bring the story to the public's eye and vindicate this assistant's work, so his death did not go in vain.

Runestones of Death

The Dublin Trio was at home relaxing when a fax came through from Romania. The curator of a Romanian museum called the Sorcerer and Magic Museum came to the horrific discovery that his tour guide had been murdered. The police knew it, but he wanted an independent analysis from someone with mystical knowledge. He asked the Dublin Trio to investigate the situation.

The Dublin Trio arrived at the museum in Romania and, to his horror, found the crime scene very unusual because runestones surrounded the body. Through his experience with spirituality, he realized there were alchemy signs written on the body. The earth sign appeared on the forehead, and the water sign appeared below the throat. The air sign was written on the heart, and the fire sign was above the belly button.

The curator told the Dublin Trio that the tour guide was working on a significant discovery to help humankind evolve to the next level of spiritual consciousness. The tour guide described this discovery as "The Ten Gates of Truth." The curator believed that someone or an organization may not have wanted this inspirational material that the tour guide was working on to reach humankind. The crime scene was perplexing due to the complexity and depth of the mysticism and spirituality present.

The Dublin trio gathered the runestones and took them to do some research. Traditionally, there were 24 runestones in each set throughout history. Runestones were created in the second century AD by the Norse religion. Each stone had its own inscription with unique meanings as an early alphabet for the Vikings, though some people say the runestones originated in Scandinavia, which is now in Denmark, and in Germany.

The odd thing was the number of runestones at the murder scene was 25, not 24.

The Dublin Trio took a closer look. One of the stones bore a swastika sticker, which made him think an organization from the Nazi party was behind the murder and had left a deliberate clue to be cocky and show off their work.

So, the Dublin Trio looked up how many Nazi organizations there were and zeroed in on one particular organization that seemed the most likely hate group. They were the Stammlager Party, a branch of the Nazi Stalin organization. The Trio arranged a meeting with the top authorities of the Nazi Stalin organization. These authorities were aware of the Dublin Trio's intentions because they had been behind the murder of the tour guide.

The Dublin Trio entered the room with the Nazi authorities and made small talk, then said, "Let me tell you why I'm here." He went into the situation at the museum and explained the mystery of the 25th runestone. He asked the authorities, "Can you please explain to me why there is a Swastika on one of the runestones surrounding the murder scene?"

The Nazis played coy, even though they knew the history of the runestones, so they said, "Can you please provide us with some wisdom on these stones?"

The Dublin Trio provided background information about the history of the runestones, but he was cunning and thinking as well, and he surmised that the authorities were not being honest with him. So, while he offered info on the runestones, he was considering open-ended questions to ask at the end that would slip them up and incriminate them.

When he finished, he asked, "In your opinion which origin of language did the inscriptions come from, Scandinavian or German?" Because the authorities said they did not know the runestones, any answer would incriminate them. However, they had not paid attention, and they answered the question with "Scandinavian."

The Dublin Trio had all he needed. These two leaders of a hate group knew about the runestones and were lying to him from the beginning. With that in him, the Trio thanked them and graciously walked out of the room, needing to digest the situation and not overreact. There was much more information to consider.

He realized that he needed to apply his attention to the next item, which is why the murder victim had four classic alchemy signs inscribed on him: earth, water, air, and fire. The Dublin Trio, being well versed in spiritual matters, understood that the history of alchemy was to purify, mature, and perfect certain materials, with a primary focus on transmuting base metals into gold. Gold meant a higher level of enlightenment in your journey with God.

The Trio started thinking, what did runestones and alchemy have to do with the murder scene, and what did they have to do with the Nazi Stalin party, who he knew was behind the murder? He sat down at the desk in his hotel room and started to ponder deeply. Soon, he came to the conclusion that because runestones and alchemy were the beginnings of spirituality, it was possible the roots of both these spiritual elements were used to taunt. The runestones and alchemy were examples to mock the origins spirituality with an incredulous, insulting display by placing them at the murder scene.

The Nazi Stalin party had to be held accountable for the murder of the tour guide. So, the Dublin Trio went back, but this time, he returned with a small tape recorder in his coat pocket to get a confession from the authorities. As he met with the Nazis, through their conversation, the Trio brought to their attention that the room where the victim was murdered was normally dimly lit, and whoever murdered him would need a decently illuminated room to write the alchemy signs on the body.

Now, the Dublin Trio knew the time of death from the coroner's report, and because of this, he knew that the room was illuminated by the sun from the east side of the room, while there were also windows on the west side that brought light in while the sun went down. Whoever murdered the tour guide benefited from the light coming in from the east side windows.

During the Dublin Trio's questioning, he asked the Nazis, "Do you know which window the sun was coming in through when you normally walked through that room?" This question was incriminating because, under normal circumstances, people were not aware of where sunlight is streaming from when they entered a room.

The Nazi authorities said, "The east window," which was the exact window the sun was illuminating on the day the tour guide was murdered. This would give the prosecution enough evidence when included with what the Dublin Trio discovered from his first conversation with them. He was satisfied that he had sufficient evidence to make a citizen's arrest on a felony charge of murder.

So, the Dublin Trio said, "By the power invested in me as a citizen in the state of Pennsylvania, you are both under arrest for the death of the tour guide in Romania." He pulled out his cell phone and called the proper authorities.

But the Nazi authorities were art collectors and displayed on the walls behind them were medieval relics, including swords and morning stars—rods with attached chains and large, spiky metal balls on the ends. They grabbed weapons and approached the Trio with the intent to murder him because he knew too much.

The Dublin Trio snatched a broom from the corner of the room, unscrewed the wooden pole, and used it to defend himself. He stood tense in the cramped office, the stale air thick with the scent of old wood and desperation. Posters of propaganda plastered the walls, remnants of a time when the Nazi Stalin party believed they could instill fear. But the Trio wasn't afraid. Not anymore.

Quickly, the Trio's eyes narrowed as he held the broomstick like a staff, ready to defend against the imminent threat.

The two agents eyed him in the far corner with surprise and malice. One held a gleaming sword, the other a morning star. "Think you can take us on, you fool?" the agent with the sword sneered, brandishing it with a flourish that was more theatrical than menacing.

"It's not the weapon's size. It's the wielder's skill!" replied the Dublin Trio, gripping his makeshift weapon tighter.

The agents charged, boots thudding against the wooden floor echoing in the small room. The sword swung through the air with a sharp whoosh, narrowly missing the Trio as he ducked and rolled to the side. The morning star's chain whistled ominously, but he was already on his feet again, the pole ready for action. "Come on!" he shouted, a grin on his face. "Is that all you've got?"

With a swift jab, he caught the sword-wielding agent in the stomach, the wooden pole making a satisfying thwack against flesh. The man doubled over, wheezing, but the second agent lunged forward, chain spinning in a deadly arc. "You think you can defeat us?" the second agent growled, swinging the chain like he was trying to catch a wild beast.

"Try me!" the Trio laughed, weaving under the swing. He turned the pole around, striking the chain with a crack that sent the metal ball flying across the room. "Ah! You little—" the agent cursed, scrambling to regain control.

The battle became chaotic, a dance of strikes and blocks, the wooden pole against ancient weapons. Their struggle filled the room, punctuated by the rhythmic clang of metal and wood.

"Is this your best? You really must be at the bottom of the class!" the Trio mocked, a playful glint in his eyes. With a swift spin, he caught the sword-wielder off guard, sending him to the floor with a thud.

The agent groaned, clutching his side, while the second agent roared in anger, swinging the chain wildly. "Stop moving, you pest!"

But the Trio was too quick, dodging and weaving until he expertly disarmed the man. The chain clattered to the ground, leaving the agent defenseless. "Citizen's arrest!" he declared, chest heaving with exertion as adrenaline coursed through him.

"You're going to regret this!" the sword-wielder spat, struggling to rise.

"Not a chance," he replied, stepping back and gesturing dramatically. "Welcome to your new home, gentlemen. I hear the accommodations are quite...cozy."

The agents exchanged worried glances, realizing they were now the prey in a game they thought they controlled. "Now, let's see how you like being on the other side," the Trio said, a triumphant grin spreading across his face as he moved to tie them up.

The Dublin Trio had faced greater challenges, but this one felt like a good small victory against the shadows creeping into their world. With a final glance at the defeated agents, he chuckled softly. "Guess you underestimated the power of a broom."

The Trio turned the Nazi Stalin agents over to the authorities. As he reflected on this case, he realized how all journeys had lessons to teach, and it was up to us to reflect on our own lives and get the most out of them.

Time Portal

The Dublin Trio's sister was visiting from out of town and staying at the Dublin Trio's house. On this particular day, the Dublin Trio was running errands. While out, he received an urgent phone call from his sister, who got a fax from a museum in Jerusalem. They wanted to hire the Dublin Trio, and when he returned home, they wanted him to call one of the top authorities at the museum to discuss the matter.

So, the Dublin Trio rushed home, called the number, and talked to the top authority at the museum, who asked the Trio if he had ever heard of the Dead Sea Scrolls. The Dublin Trio had limited knowledge, but was aware of these scrolls. The museum authority explained in confidence that they had discovered a time portal in one of the Dead Sea Scrolls caves, and he asked the Dublin Trio, who had security clearance, for his discretion on this top-secret mission.

All kinds of thoughts and intrigue entered the Dublin Trio's mind. The museum wanted the Dublin Trio to come at once to help investigate the situation. So, the Trio arrived in Jerusalem and was escorted to the caves of the Dead Sea Scrolls, where the authorities awaited him. In one of the caves is a massive blanket. They took off the blanket to reveal a huge hole with a barrier of air that seemed solid and royal blue, but crystallized.

The Dublin Trio examined the time portal and decided to stick his hand into the crystal air. His hand disappeared up to the elbow. He moved his arm in and out of the crystal air matter, testing the boundaries of the time portal and trying to examine it to the best of his ability.

Then, the authorities brought attention to the seriousness at hand, explaining they tested the time portal several days ago by throwing an empty Coke bottle. To their astonishment, the bottle came back the next day with a message, which read, "We are insurgents to the Nazi Party in 1933, and Hitler is trying to build a nuclear bomb that could devastate humanity for years to come. If he succeeds, he could alter the space-time continuum, which could affect the time mechanics between the past and the future."

The museum authorities decided this issue must be addressed, because if they didn't, Hitler could succeed in building a nuclear bomb. If he detonated it, the event could significantly alter mankind's destiny for decades. They could not allow this axis of evil to prevail. They wanted the Dublin Trio to go through the time portal, meet up with the insurgents, and stop Hitler from developing the bomb.

This was a huge decision for the Dublin Trio for several reasons. One, if he went through the portal, he was not certain it would lead him to the Nazi insurgents. Two, he felt the weight of the responsibility for stopping Hitler. However, he knew this was his job and what he signed up. So, he prepared all his gear and confidently entered the time portal.

He felt like his body had gone instantly transparent but still intact as he traveled through some type of wormhole, and his arms and legs expanded and contracted. Suddenly, his body solidified again as he entered a cave. He wandered through the cave and found what appeared to be humanoids, erect but ape-like. Most of them were around a fire.

The Dublin Trio's best deduction was that these were Neanderthals, because he knew they primarily lived in caves. He approached the clan cautiously, realizing Neanderthals in this era were very territorial. He waved gestures of peace and welcoming, but it didn't matter. The head of the Neanderthal clan menacingly approached the Trio and challenged him to a physical confrontation in order to protect the clan

The Dublin Trio understood. Nevertheless, he had to defend himself, which he did. He easily took down the head of the clan but did not hurt him. He let him back up and continued to approach the clan with gestures of peace and welcoming, arms stretched wide in a message of hope.

As the clan realized this stranger had taken down their toughest member, they regarded him with respect and offered him a piece of bison as a gesture of peace. While eating the bison, he noticed the clan looking at the gear he brought with him. They had never seen such material before, like the rappelling rope and carabiners attached to his waist.

He thought it might be a good opportunity to teach the Neanderthals how to rappel down a mountain before he left them. He thought that would be a good life experience for them as they went forward in their journey. So, through hand gestures and other forms of communication, the Dublin Trio indicated that he wanted to teach them.

They chose a cliff, and the Neanderthals watched intently as he used the rope to rappel down to the bottom, and then ascend to the top. After a few demonstrations, the Neanderthals picked up the ability to repel, and they were grateful to the Dublin Trio for teaching them this new skill.

Feeling good about himself, that he left something positive behind, he decided it was time to reenter the portal and return to his original mission. He returned and walked deep into the cave, searching for the time portal. Realizing that the portal was a mechanism of temporal mechanics, he started thinking that because there was energy in speech, if he said something like *Portal*, the connection between energy, time, and quantum mechanics would coalesce and the voice command should work.

So, he yelled out urgently, "Portal!" And the time portal opened up there on the cave wall. He went through it again, and this time, he ended up in a Nazi prison camp in a squadron's cabin. When he appeared, he once again made welcoming and peace gestures to the American prisoners who were all seated at a table.

The American captain said, "We were hoping someone would arrive. We sent the Coke bottle back with the note" The Dublin Trio recognized the captain's credentials, then saluted him and identified himself. "Ryan Shamus, reporting as recruited, lieutenant of the 3rd Battalion of the Green Berets Special Ops. At your service."

The captain saluted him and said, "Great, we have plenty of work to do." The captain, his squadron, and the Trio sat around a table, and the captain spoke. "Okay, Dublin Trio, from what we understand, the nuclear bomb is being built in the rocket propulsion lab in Nazi Germany, and it must be stopped. This bomb can't fall into the hands of a regime that advocates such evilness."

"So, here's my plan. Tonight, at the weakest spot in the prison wall surveillance, you're going to climb the wall and escape, then find your way to Nazi headquarters. Here's a Nazi officers uniform so you can assimilate once you get there, work your way toward the rocket propulsion lab, and destroy the nuclear bomb."

The Dublin Trio knew his responsibilities. He rappelled up the prison wall late at night, then escaped into deep forest foliage. He found a train idling on tracks and determined that its destination was Nazi headquarters. So, he jumped into an abandoned car and changed into his Nazi uniform on the way. When he arrived, he jumped out of the train car, only to be met by two curious guards. But since the Dublin Trio's rank was superior, they quickly deferred to him and guided him to the rocket propulsion lab.

The Dublin Trio entered the lab and told the scientists they were needed at an important meeting regarding their work, so the scientists left. Then, he went about his business disabling the nuclear bomb, which he accomplished quickly. Then, he realized the cold concrete walls of the rocket propulsion lab echoed with the faint hiss of steam and the distant hum of machinery. Flickering fluorescent lights bathed the interior in an eerie glow, casting long shadows.

The Dublin Trio stood alone amid the chaos. He had just disabled the nuclear bomb, but the victory was short-lived. The clatter of boots on the floor announced the approach of two guards, their nightsticks glinting ominously under the fluorescent lights.

"Did you hear that?" one guard said, a sneer creeping across his face.

"Yeah. I think we found our little saboteur," the other replied, his voice dripping with menace.

The Trio scanned the area, his heart racing. He spotted a piece of iron pipe on the ground—a makeshift weapon. Upon grabbing it, he felt a surge of adrenaline.

The guards were closing in, their confidence palpable. "Think you can take us?" one guard taunted, cracking his knuckles.

"Just try," he shot back, his voice steady, betraying none of the fear churning inside.

With a swift movement, the guards lunged forward, nightsticks raised. The Trio ducked and swung the pipe, connecting with one guard's knee. A sharp crack rang through the air, and the guard released a howl of pain. "Argh! You little—"

But before he could finish, the second guard swung his stick. The Trio barely managed to sidestep, but the impact sent him sprawling to the ground. Breathless, he rolled and sprang back up, determination igniting within him. "Not today!" he shouted, echoing through the lab.

He charged forward, the pipe raised high. The first guard, still nursing his knee, scrambled to his feet, but the Trio was quicker. He swung the pipe again, catching the guard squarely in the ribs. The guard grunted and doubled over, gasping for breath.

"Come on, you call that a fight?" the Trio taunted, his confidence growing.

The second guard, furious now, charged, his nightstick aimed at the Trio's head. With a deft sidestep, the Trio dodged, then swung the pipe in a broad arc, knocking the weapon from the guard's hands. The guard stumbled back, panic flashing in his eyes. "Is this what the Reich believes in?" he spat out, struggling to regain his footing.

He unleashed his martial arts training on the guards with a swift series of punches and expertly timed moves. A jab to the jaw sent one guard sprawling to the floor, while another quick kick sent the second guard crashing into a nearby table. Tools clattered to the ground with a cacophony of noise. "Ugh!" The second guard groaned, trying to rise but failing.

The Trio stood over them, breathless but victorious, the pipe held like a trophy. Needing an escape, he called out, "Portal!" and the time portal appeared. He entered it with his objective accomplished.

When he met the museum authorities at the end of the portal in the current time, they discussed what it all meant together. With the initial bottle being thrown through the time portal and the American prisoners tossing it back to them with a note asking for help in dismantling the nuclear bomb offset the future implications for humanity? And how it could disrupt the time displacement of future events? If Hitler had succeeded in detonating that nuclear bomb back in 1933, it would have set humanity back for hundreds of years to come.

Thank God for the brave American prisoners who were doing their duty when they sent back the bottle with information about Hitler's intentions. Let their patriotic sacrifice ring from sea to shining sea, and let it be a symbol of all the sacrifices that have been made in the spirit of liberty and freedom.